# CURSE OF THE PHARAOH'S MANICURISTS
## (WITHYCOMBE AND DOYLE, BOOK 1)

# CURSE OF THE PHARAOH'S MANICURISTS
# (WITHYCOMBE AND DOYLE, BOOK 1)


By
Nick Rowan

DREAMING BIG
PUBLICATIONS

*A large thank you to my Patreon patrons: Laura, Drew, Damit, Rose, Kiwi, Elizabeth, Cindy and Sarah.*

# CHAPTER 1

# LORD WITHYCOMBE'S SECRETARY

**It** was with modest trepidation and a good deal more brazenness on a fine April day in 1923 that I approached the New York office of Edward Francis Kilsby, Lord Withycombe, renowned flying ace of the Great War and adventurer extraordinaire. For myself, I was barely twenty-two and the ink had scarcely dried on my journalism degree from the hallowed halls of Dartmouth.

—From the journal of Charles Doyle, secretary to Lord Withycombe

***

Charlie Doyle checked the address on the newspaper ad against the one on the building, 2347 Elm. This was it. He plucked up his courage which was already strained to the breaking point, resettled his round glasses on his nose and climbed the stairs to the office where he knocked on the door. The name "Withycombe Enterprises, Ltd." sparkled on the glass, freshly painted in a gleaming gold. Charlie swallowed hard at the name, familiar from numerous news articles. The article had given only the address, not a name. Here went nothing.

"Come in!"

He stepped into the dim office. The wavy-haired man behind the desk never looked up. Charlie stood patiently for a minute, watching the way the light coming through the flyspecked windowpane picked out golden highlights in his light brown hair. He looked just like all his pictures in the paper, a few years older than the young flying ace who had dazzled the world, barely thirty if Charlie's memory served, but still just as handsome, perhaps more so for having grown into his nose and chin.

Then Charlie cleared his throat.

"I'm quite aware of you, young man. Sit down and I'll be ready in a moment." The very posh British accent told Charlie he might be playing out of his league.

Charlie sat in one of the stiff wooden chairs and read the ad again silently as he tried not to fidget. "Wanted, eager young secretary to pursue adventure, wealth, and glory. Travel mandatory. Orphans preferred. English or Journalism degree and passport required."

He pushed his glasses up his nose and watched the man's big hands shuffle papers as he read and then stacked them. From time to time, a frown made his thin mustache turn down. Charlie suspected he'd already blown the interview. That wouldn't be the worst thing that could happen to him. Ever since he'd seen the ad, his head had been filled with tales from pulp serials about lurid adventures in jungle cities and stand-offs with impossible creatures in tight situations. His more pragmatic side had asked exactly where they would be traveling, whether he would be able to get home in case of emergency and what the food would be like. He had awakened from a nasty nightmare about nearly dying of a broken leg in a lost cave while rats gnawed on him in the darkness. That had almost been enough to dissuade him. Almost.

After a several minutes, perhaps a quarter of an hour, the man looked up, his stern eyes catching Charlie's and holding him trapped in his chair. Surely the man could see every thought in his head.

"Very well. I am Edward Kilsby, Lord Withycombe. At the moment, I'm unsure you're suited to the rigors of the position."

"I meet all your requirements," Charlie protested, sitting up a little straighter. "Eager, young, journalism degree." He tried his most winning smile. "And willing to travel and pursue wealth and adventure. I even have the passport." He had acquired it the year before, thinking to visit Paris, where all of the important writing was happening these days.

Lord Withycombe looked him over again, scrutinizing him with rather more care than Charlie thought was necessary. The penetrating gaze traveled over him with nearly palpable weight, taking in every aspect and daring him to flinch from the examination. The unnerving inspection went on far too long and Charlie fought not to blush. He had felt less naked sitting on the doctor's table, even though he was fully dressed. "You do appear to be in good health," he conceded.

"In the pink." Charlie barely restrained himself from thumping his chest. "What is it they say in the baby-milk ads? For strength and vigor, I defy the world." Charlie knew as soon as the words were out of his mouth that it had been the wrong thing to say. He read all of the newspaper, of course, trying to hone his own wordsmithing skills.

Lord Withycombe looked at him, an odd and unreadable expression on his face, and nodded slowly. "I'll take your word for that." He shuffled a few more papers, staring at Charlie with cold eyes, as if daring him to squirm. "I will give you the opportunity to prove yourself over three months. I like your enthusiasm."

Charlie smiled widely at that. "When do I start, Lord Withycombe?"

"Tomorrow." Lord Withycombe handed him a sheet of paper and a fat wallet.

Charlie peeked in and saw what looked like a couple of couple of hundred dollars in cash. The paper had a list of clothing and supplies that was, brief, concise, and nearly illegible.

"These are the things you will need. Meet me here tomorrow at six in the morning, ready to travel. I've wasted a great deal of time finding the right man for this position. Don't make me regret my choice."

Charlie, still half-dazed from the small fortune he held, read the list again. "Yes, sir. Bright and early tomorrow morning, all packed. I'll be here." He stood and thrust out his hand to shake, but hesitated, wondering if that was how he was supposed to take his leave of a nobleman.

Lord Withycombe stood up and shook the offered hand with a firm grip. Charlie thought he saw the beginnings of a smile lurking around the edges of the man's face.

Charlie gave him a big grin, hoping to coax it out. When the smile was not forthcoming, he left to do his shopping. He heard Lord Withycombe grumble, "Americans," behind him as the door shut.

He paused on the stairs, breathing deeply of the stale, dusty air, taking a few moments to calm himself. He had never been so glad baggy trousers were fashionable. If he had suspected Lord Withycombe had seen him get aroused just from a handshake, as well as all the observing, he'd have left the wallet, too embarrassed to return. He was in it now, and he had no idea how he would manage three months, or even a permanent posting with a man who made him feel all hot and cold and fizzy inside at the same time, as if someone had poured him a hot chocolate soda.

Now, he leaned against the wall of the stairwell, grinning as he remembered the feel of Lord Withycombe's hand, the not-quite-there smile and the scent of the man. He imagined it again, all leather and tobacco with a hint of woods and sweet cookies.

Then Charlie collected his wits, counted the money, and went shopping.

The next morning, Charlie presented himself at the office, carpetbag in one hand, typewriter case in the other. He had added a few personal items to Lord Withycombe's packing list. He wasn't going anywhere without his journal or his typewriter. Let Lord Withycombe protest, he'd use it as a seat cushion if he had to. He hoped it wouldn't end his employment, but he was prepared to explain quickly or repay the thirty dollars he had spent getting ready. The typewriter was his memento of his family and lucky charm all in one, and like many writers, he was fussy about using only his own machine.

"Good morning, young man." Lord Withycombe strolled up, his suit and tie immaculate and his own carpetbag bulging. He glared at the typewriter case. "I believe my list said only the items on it."

"Yes, Lord Withycombe. But if you want a proper secretary, I'll need my typewriter." He held his breath and waited to hear if he was fired before they had begun.

"I had planned to provide one later in the journey rather than cart yours halfway around the world." He shrugged and hailed a taxicab. "It makes no difference to me. If you are more comfortable with your own, please bring it. I do know secretaries and their machines. Now, all haste. The ship departs in an hour."

Charlie offered back the purse. He had been as frugal as possible in his shopping. "There's about a hundred and fifty dollars left."

Edward opened the door of the cab. "About thirty pounds. Which is your monthly salary. Keep the purse, and consider it your first month's pay."

Charlie tucked away the money, picked up his bags, and followed his new employer into the cab. Apparently, his lordship wasn't the stiff Charlie had thought. A hard man would have fired him on the spot for the typewriter, and taken back the purse as well. Rules could be bent if there was a valid reason, it seemed. Now, all he had to do was either not get caught getting up to trouble, or have a really good answer when he was.

When they arrived at the docks, Charlie looked at the great steamship, amazed as the sheer immensity of it. Although he lived in the city, he never had cause to come here. He'd always imagined ships as the small things depicted in history books, but this looked like a skyscraper on the water.

The great black hull swooped high above his head to the whitewashed deck and railing. The towering smokestack sent a cloud puffing skyward. People waved from the deck to other people on the dock below.

He suddenly realized he had stopped walking to gawk, and Lord Withycombe's long stride was carrying him up the gangway… without Charlie.

Charlie hurried after his employer, ignoring the other passengers in their summer linens and gauzy dresses. He clutched his valise and typewriter tightly and made judicious use of his elbows, finally catching up with his employer at the purser's desk.

The purser handed Lord Withycombe his keys. Charlie followed him down a few decks to their suite. It was about the size of Charlie's old apartment, big enough for a bed, a sofa and a very tiny head built into the bulkhead. Charlie looked out the porthole and over the dock, realizing he was about three stories high.

Lord Withycombe cleared his throat and settled into the lone chair with his newspaper. Charlie took the hint and scurried about, putting things away. He bit back the thousands of questions he was bursting to ask. The *London Times* made a formidable moat and wall against impertinent interruptions.

Finished, he settled down with his own journal to record his first impressions of the ship. He wrote a page and found his prose drifting to Lord Withycombe. He wrote about his employer's hands holding the paper, the faint smell of his pipe, and his slow, even breathing.

Charlie stopped writing. He'd lost his train of thought anyway. He reread what he had written and winced. He sounded moony and soppy. But it was there on the page and he didn't cross it out. He just observed instead of writing, and tried to focus on the ship. In college, he'd been too busy for much of a love life. He'd always loved dancing and had no trouble finding a girl to take to the school dances. But he'd never gone steady or gotten serious with any of them.

However, there had been one roommate, a quiet boy named Frank who greatly admired the lifestyle of the Romantic poets and imitated them upon every possible occasion. They had gotten tight on a small flask of bootleg absinthe one evening and Frank had kissed him, calling him Shelley. In return, since the kiss wasn't awful, Charlie had kissed Frank, calling him Byron.

He thought of Frank now as Lord Withycombe lowered the paper. He wondered what it would be like to kiss a man with a mustache. He wondered, too, how unethical his thoughts would be considered. He reminded himself to pay close attention, stay respectful and not get distracted.

"So, I suspect, Mr. Doyle, you're wondering why we're in second class?"

Charlie blushed a little to be caught lost in inappropriate thoughts. He took a breath, trying to stop. He hated the way he blushed at the slightest provocation. "Yes, Lord Withycombe. But I'm sure you have your reasons."

"In first class, I get introduced to half a dozen women's daughters. Or more. Sometimes introduced multiple times, depending on how much sherry their mothers have had." He gave a rakish grin. "In point of fact, I am the most eligible bachelor in England." He rolled his eyes at the phrase, a look of extreme boredom on his face, and Charlie could almost read the social column he had lifted it from. "So, since I value my privacy, this little cabin provides me with the peace and quiet I require for comfortable travel."

"I'm afraid I'll be disturbing your peace and quiet, your lordship. I snore," Charlie confessed.

"That's not a problem, Mr. Doyle. I shall simply smother you with a pillow if need be."

Charlie's eyes went big and he covered his mouth with his hands. "I'll do my best not to, sir."

Lord Withycombe chuckled and leaned forward with a soft laugh. "I'm joking, Charles. Although, the fellows in my regiment did try that on me back in '17. I snore rather like a Handley-Page, myself, or so the old regiment claimed. The aerodrome chaps they brought in had a bitter argument as to whether it was a Handley-Page or a Sopwith Camel."

Charlie wasn't sure if this was another joke, since Lord Withycombe still had a straight face. He turned to a safer subject. "Did you fly a Sopwith, sir?" he asked, leaning forward a little himself. He'd followed the War in the papers, obsessed with flying at thirteen and fourteen. Airplanes were still uncommon in civilian life, although air mail had been established about six years before. Charlie dearly hoped at some point he would get to fly.

"Oh yes. Flew one and bought her off the RAF with my wartime pay. You'll get to see her." He shook his head and lit his pipe. "She's a single-seater, though, and deucedly temperamental, so I won't be flying us to Paris in her."

"Fly? Paris?" Charlie knew he was being incoherent. His impossible wish was about to be granted, in a way he never dreamed. "I… I never expected—"

"Oh, yes. It's a very pleasant trip in the spring." Lord Withycombe smiled, looking nostalgic. "I haven't been for about five years."

Charlie collected himself quickly. "Very good, sir. I'm looking forward to it. That's why I got the passport originally. All the really important writing is being done in Paris." The ship's engines grew louder and the vessel lurched a little. Charlie looked at Lord Withycombe and gave him a smile as he reopened his journal.

"And so begins my first adventure in the company of the renowned Edward Kilsby, Lord Withycombe," he said, writing as he spoke.

"Very good, I like the sound of my name from you, Charles. Please continue to use it. This should be a quiet trip. Adventure at sea sometimes quickly turns into tragedy. We can both do without that quite nicely."

"Yes sir, Edward." Charlie tried out the new form of address. It sounded very nice coming out of his mouth. Very nice indeed. He stared at his journal for a moment more, but as the ship surged and rocked out of the harbor, he felt quite odd.

"Answer me one thing, Charles," Lord Withycombe said in a voice that would tolerate no nonsense.

Charlie looked up and nodded.

"What was it about my advertisement that made you answer it? Was it the adventure?"

Charlie nodded and tried to look serious. "I haven't done anything exciting in my life. Just school and more school." The high point had been working on *The Dartmouth*, a paper founded by Daniel Webster himself. He didn't think his employer would be interested in that bit of trivia.

Before he could say more, a tap at the door announced the chambermaid. The little redhead was what the boys at Charlie's school had called "pleasingly plump," not fat but very curvy and heavier than the boyish figures that were just now coming into vogue. She gave a little curtsy and held up an armful of towels.

"There's an en suite bath, your lordship," she said. "And they told me you needed an extra pillow and blanket for your servant."

"Secretary," Charlie and Edward corrected.

She dropped a deeper curtsy and giggled. "Yes, your lordship." She put the towels away and ducked out for a moment.

Charlie watched Lord Withycombe watching her round little bottom as she put the blanket on the bottom shelf of a wall-mounted table. He had to admit, it was an attractive rear. He bet it would feel nice in his hands.

Lord Withycombe beckoned her closer. She came to him. He caught her hand and pulled her close to whisper. Charlie strained to hear, but her giggling covered everything except five heavy clinks, like large coins being dropped in her hand. He listened to his own insides gurgling, a bit louder than the lap of water outside the ship.

"I understand, Lord Withycombe," she said. She curtsied one last time and ducked out, her pretty freckles not hiding her own blush.

Withycombe watched as she left. "They've changed the uniforms a little. I approve," he said to himself, before returning to Charlie. "There will be plenty of adventure, if you don't get bored with the preliminaries."

"I've never been on a ship before." Charlie tried to write and his journal lurched appallingly.

"Indeed. You look quite green, Charles. The porthole's too high for the necessity. You'd better head for the deck."

Charlie tried to stand up, but sank back, shakily. "I'm not feeling well at all, sir. Maybe I'd better go to bed." His stomach flipped and he found his feet, fleeing for the deck, glad he'd been too excited to eat more than a roll for breakfast.

The roiling of the ocean in the wake of the ship mirrored the roiling of Charlie's insides. He bent over the rail twice, then sat in a deck chair for a few minutes. A passing steward took pity on him and returned with a cool glass of soda water.

The fizziness of the drink soothed him, but when he belched, he had to run for the rail again. He finally returned to the cabin, pale, clammy, and exhausted.

Withycombe was just finishing a pipe and looked up. "Better?" He knocked the ashes from the pipe and set it near the ashtray. "It appears not," he amended when he saw Charlie's sweaty face.

"Better," Charlie croaked. "I'm just not feeling up to par."

He nodded. "You'll get your sea legs shortly."

Charlie, shaking from the heaves, bundled up in the blanket the maid had left. "If you have no further need of me, sir, I think a nap might be in order."

Withycombe rose. "Go right ahead, Charles. I'll go out and see if I can find anything interesting on this ship. Have a good sleep. I'll wake you for dinner."

Charlie groaned at the thought of food.

# Curse of the Pharoah's Manicurist

*****

Withycombe did check back about dinner, but Charlie barely woke up and only waved him away weakly, not caring that this was probably not the way to inform the man that he was uninterested in food. The visit disturbed Charlie enough that his shaky stomach sent him topside again.

On the way back, he heard Withycombe's voice, followed by the most inviting laugh in the world. He walked toward the sensual sound, cautious of his wobbly legs. The maid's giggle, cute and unmistakable, joined it. He paused in front of the closet where the sounds seemed to be emanating from and listened.

His employer sighed softly and Charlie heard a great deal of rhythmic thumping. He realized what they must be doing. The maid gasped. Despite his illness, he imagined the scene and blushed hotter than his chills should have allowed.

The maid giggled again and Charlie heard Withycombe cooing to her. He walked on, uncertain if the burning in his stomach was seasickness or envy. More, he was unsure who the envy was for. He hurried back to the cabin and curled up in a ball on the sofa, pulling the blanket up. He tried to sleep but the motion of the ship and his own imagination conspired to keep him awake.

He rolled over to face the back of the couch and tried thinking in lists. He'd developed the habit to fall asleep as a child. He could often fall asleep by Martin van Buren. On nights that didn't work, he went to rulers of England. It was a rare night he got as far back as Cromwell.

It was only when a soft voice, accompanied by a light being kindled, asked, "Mr. Doyle? Are you well?" that Charlie realized he was no longer alone.

"Millard Fillmore," he blurted. He wanted to sink right through the divan and the deck and all the other decks and the hull and walk home along the bottom of the ocean floor. His face burned like a red-hot coal in the dim cabin.

"Oh no," he moaned. "I'm sorry, sir."

Withycombe frowned and looked a bit puzzled. "It's all right, Charles. But Millard Fillmore?."

"I recite the presidents in reverse order to help fall asleep, sir. You startled me. I'm sorry. I'm an idiot."

To his surprise, Withycome smiled. "That's a clever trick you have. They trained us to fall asleep quickly in the War, because quiet moments were a rare and precious thing and sleep was sometimes hard to come by. I was never very good at it. Are you feeling any better?"

"Only a bit, sir." Charlie pulled the blanket back up to his chin. The cabin was cooler than he'd expected, but his face still glowed with a blush. He'd been useless, seasick, and rude, but Lord Withycombe didn't seem to mind. Edward patted him gently on the head.

"Rest a bit longer, Charles." Withycombe laid a hand across his forehead, as if checking for fever. "I'll return later."

Charlie nestled deeper into the blanket when the cabin door shut. He was alone again in the rapidly darkening cabin.

*****

It was full dark before Withycombe returned, smoking his pipe and looking quite pleased. Charlie was sitting up, with only a single lamp lit, and sipping at a soda water he'd finagled from a passing porter. He tried not to blush.

"Feeling better, Charles?" Withycombe asked as he turned up the lights.

"Yes, sir. I think I'm all empty." Charlie got up and rummaged in his carpetbag. "Sir, I hate to say this, but your packing list has a deficiency. And I forgot to add my own pajamas."

"I'm sure I have a spare." He dug in his own carpetbag. "I apologize, the list was written a bit hastily." He found what he was looking for and him a heavy, striped nightshirt. "Quite."

"I apologize, sir. I'm sorry to be such a nuisance. It's unprofessional. My only excuse is that I'm not quite myself." Charlie slipped into the nightshirt. His employer was a tall man and Charlie stood slightly below average. He flopped in the nightshirt, his hands lost in the sleeves. What should have been knee-length came below his calves and the neck slit plunged much too deep for decency, or warmth. He briefly considered asking for a safety pin, or adding a button in the morning.

"Oh dear." Withycombe had popped his own nightshirt on, giving Charlie a glimpse of a tattoo on his chest, and came over to help Charlie sort himself out. "Well, it works in a pinch. You're decent and won't have to sleep in your clothes." He started rolling the other of Charlie's sleeves up.

Charlie finally cuffed the other one to his satisfaction, not feeling well enough to be curious about the brief peek. He filed it for later. "Do you read before bed or are we going right to sleep?" He really didn't want to try reading right now.

"Straight to sleep, I think. Although there will be nights when I do read. Try to get some rest, Charles."

"Thank you, sir." Charlie curled up on the sofa with the blanket and pillow. He bundled into the blanket, half-afraid he'd be sent back home on the first ship. He hadn't had a very good first day.

"You're welcome, Charles." Withycombe doused the lights and got into bed.

*****

Charlie did not sleep well, his agitated stomach sending him to the rail several times, despite his earlier assertions of being empty. He suspected he woke his employer with at least one of his late forays, but the man said nothing. Charlie was up at dawn, sipping soda water and writing in his journal while feeling very dragged out, when Withycombe woke.

"Hard night, Charles?" his employer asked as he rose and stretched, then began his morning ablutions.

"Yes, sir, sorry. I must have disturbed you." Charlie became acutely aware he hadn't yet shaved or combed his hair.

"It's perfectly all right. I don't suppose you want breakfast?" Withycombe finished lathering up with the mug and brush and started shaving.

Charlie felt the blood drain out of his face as his mouth went dry at the sight. No matter how sick he was, he was still on a journey with a most attractive man. He sipped some more soda water. It seemed to help. "Toast, maybe? Please? I don't think I can handle the dining room."

"I'll bring breakfast here." His lordship dressed leisurely, and retied his tie twice.

Charlie, wrapped in a blanket as a dressing gown, drank more soda water. His fingers itched to fix it. He could do it quicker and more neatly. "I'm sorry to be such a nuisance. I feel all scraped out."

"Poor lad. The ship hasn't treated you very well so far." Withycombe knotted his tie to his satisfaction and then shot Charlie a sympathetic smile.

"How do you travel so easily, sir?"

"Practice, all my life." He looked Charlie over and nodded as he headed to the door. "I'll get you your toast. See if you have better luck with it."

"Thank you. When I'm not so green, I'll wait on you." While Lord Withycombe was gone, he wrote more in his journal, mostly about Edward, how handsome and kind and generous his employer was.

Withycombe came back with a tray containing toast and tea, some butter, and several kinds of jam. There was a slice of cheese and some tomatoes as well, but Charlie didn't want them. Withycombe scooped up that plate himself, added a few slices of toast, and smeared them liberally with jam.

"The end of my own breakfast," he explained, taking a bite of the cheese.

"You didn't have to interrupt it for me," Charlie said, picking up a piece of dry toast and nibbling the corner. He waited to see if he could tolerate it and ate half of a slice. He sipped a cup of tea. "Thank you. It was a difficult night."

"I could tell." Withycombe took up a book he'd brought in with him. "The ship's library is fairly stocked. If you want something in particular, I can get it for you."

"I'll look into it when I feel better, thanks." Charlie sipped more tea and caught the subtle scrutiny he was under. "So, my lord, what are we to do this trip? It's several days to London." He frowned at that. Several days in constant discomfort would be unpleasant and get them off on a bad foot. "Do I interview you for posterity or what?"

"We could at that. Get a head start on that biography." Withycom set the book down and chuckled.

Charlie looked at him, a bit flabbergasted. "I'm to write your biography? Wouldn't it be a memoir? Or shall I just ghost and call it an autobiography?" He took a sip of the tea to collect his wits and stop babbling. "I mean,

I had no idea what being your secretary would consist of, except taking correspondence."

Withycombe nodded. "Eventually, it was a project I thought I'd like to explore. It's why I asked for the journalism degree, after all. But I don't feel as if my exploits are over yet. There's far more to do."

Charlie tried to look as excited as his exhaustion and lingering queasiness allowed. "I look forward to them. And to being the one who records them."

"Oh, you like that idea. Good. I hoped you would."

"A book and more adventures. I mean, we hear about you in the newspapers from time to time. Less now that the War is over. I think… I wonder…" Charlie pondered a moment. "Hmm. I don't know anyone who could make it, but I bet you'd be a smash as a newsreel. Frank Buck always is. The stuff about him from that new zoo in San Diego is just amazing."

Withycombe gave him a charming grin and made himself comfortable and started his pipe. "What do they say about me across the pond, I wonder? I wasn't in New York long enough to read anything or visit the cinema."

Charlie picked up his writing pad. "The stories are about the treasure you've found, the wild places you've been. There are a couple of guys writing pulp fiction about you."

Withycombe laughed, really laughed, at that. The sound filled the little cabin and set Charlie's skin afire. It crawled over him like a tangible thing, making him want to join right in. It was a sound meant for a bigger space and it fit this large-than-life. "Well, we'll simply have to outdo them,." he declared.

Charlie licked the tip of his pencil and said, "I suspect the real adventures don't involve mummies and lost cities and a single bullet in your revolver as often as theirs do."

"No. I never start out without at least three bullets ready." Withycombe gave him an impish smile. "The truth is always better than fiction."

Feeling much restored by the tea, Charlie took another cup of it. "Besides, you have me now. Worst comes to worst, I can beat the monster back with my typewriter."

"Deadly instrument, that. Lethal in the right hands."

Charlie giggled a little, caught himself, and realized his employer wasn't actually joking. "So... biography it is. Part one, at least. All right. Shall we do it Dickensian or Pepys? Or shall I be Boswell to your Johnson?"

"I prefer something entirely new. Your own style."

Charlie shook his head. "I only meant, do you want to start with 'I am born and raised,' or shall I just keep a journal and work from that?"

"I think a journal with some memories, as I recall them." He considered a long while. "Starting at the beginning would be terribly boring. I did almost nothing of interest for a full four or five years."

Charlie sipped more tea and tried another slice of toast. The first was riding quite well, but his stomach was growling for more. "It's only boring when you live it." He made himself more comfortable. "All right, if we're starting off with childhood, give me one really good childhood adventure."

Withycombe settled back in his chair, deep in thought and smiled. "That would probably be the day I took my father's best horse with the intent of running away."

"Oh my. Horse thieving is still a hanging offense back home." Charlie scribbled down the words "stole father's best horse as child."

"Yes, but I was young Master Edward and somehow thought that even striking out on my own, I was still entitled to my inheritance. In this case, that horse. Old Barbara…" He remembered the name with no fondness in his voice at all. "She was a chestnut mare, seven years old. And she had little tolerance for anyone but my father. Most grooms couldn't handle her. She got perhaps three or four miles down the road and she started rebelling. She tried to brush me off her back at a few trees, and when she couldn't be rid of me that way, she reared high and threw me off. Unfortunately, my clothes were tangled up in some of the buckles and she threw me, but not my very well-worn trousers which parted company at the seams from the force."

Charlie laughed at that image and then covered his mouth.

He continued the story, seeming not to notice the interruption. "She ran all the way back home with the shreds of them caught on her saddle. And I had to make the very cold walk back without them. It started drizzling halfway home—a cold, miserable sort of thing, not quite mist and not quite rain. I was soaked to the skin and my knees were nearly blue when I got to the house."

"Oh my. And the spanking at home?" Charlie assumed there would be one, as there had been the day he had run away from home and made his mother cry and worry.

"The thrashing was worse than the fall, yes. My father was never slack about the cane." He grinned as if it had all been a grand lark. His face darkened a bit. "I caught a ferocious case of *La Grippe* in the rain and spent the next fortnight in bed."

"Poor Young Master Edward." Charlie sighed. "Did a sympathetic maid sneak you buns for dinner after the thrashing?"

"Unfortunately not. I was a holy terror and had no sympathy at all with any of the staff. Especially not the maid, who hated my room for the odds and ends she would find there; anything from a dead frog to a live hedgehog."

"A hedgehog?" Charlie looked at him. "You kept a hedgehog?"

"Only for a day. They're very prickly pets."

Charlie noted that turn of phrase and sighed. "I was meek and quiet. I couldn't see beyond my arm and was rather timid until my parents figured out that I needed glasses." He pushed his glasses up his nose.

"They look very studious on you. It fits." Withycombe leaned in closer and whispered conspiratorially, "I'm still rumored to be a bit of a holy terror. So I need a studious secretary at my side to keep me in line."

Charlie blushed, just enough to turn pink, and shook his head, uncomprehending. "How is that going to help? It's not as if I dare stop any of your terror."

"It balances, you see. You will be there, reminding me that I have to do this and that and that it's not a good idea to… misbehave," he made that last word impossibly suggestive, and Charlie's toes curled.

Rather than encouraging his employer to misbehave, Charlie took a large of drink of tea. It helped. After a big breath, he asked, "So what are we doing, sir? I packed up and followed you aboard, with barely time for a farewell telegram to my parents."

"Well, we are headed to London where we will enjoy a few social gatherings and I will find men to hire me. To do something. Anything. We'll see when they tell me what needs doing. Enjoy the trip, Charles." He tucked his now-cold pipe in his pocket, and left the cabin. Charlie went over his notes and drank more tea, trying to sort out his own mind.

# CHAPTER 2

# ON THE LOOSE
# IN LONDON

**The** voyage across "The Pond," as Lord Withycombe calls it, was fairly uneventful. Our cabin was comfortable, the food was plentiful and good quality, and the company was most agreeable. Lord Withycombe is a very educated man. Although my own education is not lacking by American standards, when compared to such a man of the world, it is thoroughly eclipsed. Of an evening, I would join him at the rail of the ship and watch the sun set as he smoked. I did not acquire a taste for it, despite several attempts.

—From the journal of Charles Doyle, secretary to Lord Withycombe

*****

They docked at Bristol and took the Great Western Railway across to London. When they arrived at Paddington Station, Withycombe excused himself to find a telephone. Charlie sat with the bags, worn out from the hundred-mile journey and the way England seemed to pitch and roll under his feet. From Paddington Station, they took a local train to Harlow. At the Harlow station, a very young man standing beside an open auto greeted them with a bow. Charlie read the words "Crossley Manchester" on the chassis and admired the way the sun gleamed on the polished fenders.

"Good evening, my lord. Mr. Doyle. The General has some dinner ready." He gave them a bright smile, picked up the bags and put them in the boot. Charlie set his typewriter in himself.

He hesitated at the car door. His employer was already comfortable in the posh red leather backseat. He wasn't sure where he was supposed to ride. He sincerely hoped it wasn't the running board. He wasn't sure there would be room with the spare tire already there.

"Get in here, Charles." Withycombe patted the seat beside him. "Robert doesn't need you up there, getting under his gearshift."

Charlie climbed in and tried not to sit too close. The car rolled out of the village and through the countryside. Charlie watched. It looked much as most of England had, very green, with lots of low walls and rows of trees. The open spaces were a little intimidating to a city boy like him.

Robert turned off the road onto a gravel drive through a wide park. Horse chestnuts and oak trees lined the drive and darkened the evening. Charlie sat up straighter when Robert clicked on the headlights, wanting to see more. They came around the bend to where a large gray stone manor house loomed against the deepening sky. Poplars lined the long circular drive and a huge rose bed stood in the middle of the lawn, the first buds starting to show red and white and yellow.

Ivy crept along the walls, nearly reaching the roof. Three holly bushes on either side of the entrance splashed the red of their berries against the gloom.

Charlie took in the three-story house with its great tower and wings to either side and managed to say, "Wow." He was dying to explore. He wondered what Withycombe kept in the glass wing off to the east. It looked like a greenhouse. A huge and ornate cage rusted on the lawn beside it.

His employer shrugged. "It's not too large as country houses go, Charles. Nothing like where I grew up. But we sold that one years ago, couldn't afford the upkeep. We moved in with Grandfather." He saw where Charlie was looking. "My grandfather collected exotic species. He kept monkeys in that cage."

"I like monkeys," Charlie said, still staring around himself.

"I don't. Vicious, smelly, hairy brutes. I do hunt sometimes, Charles, and you'll likely get to encounter a few in the wild."

Charlie gawked at the house as Robert pulled to a stop before the front door. "Ten times as big as my folks' place. You have any sisters?" He wasn't trying to leer at that notion, but he knew he came off badly, the joke going sour.

They Edward climbed out. "One, actually. But already spoken for, sorry to say." He shot Charlie a cheerful grin.

Charlie blushed a little and mumbled, not meaning to be overheard, "Any brothers?" When Withycombe glanced his way, he added, "I have two sisters and a brother."

"I'm the eldest and only son of the ancient and noble house of Withycombe." He headed up the front stairs. "Which these days means little to nothing at all."

Robert got their bags. Charlie, ever protective of his machine, carried the typewriter up the steps hmself. A solidly-built lady of about sixty, in a gray dress and white apron, greeted them in the foyer.

"Good to have you home, my lord. Supper is ready when you are. There's water if you and your secretary would like a wash, and I've aired out a room for him adjoining yours." She gave him a maternal smile. "I know you'll have the poor lad up at all hours, since your own are hardly regular."

He gave her a smile and a quick, completely inappropriate hug. "Yes, ma'am, General Elizabeth. I've already brutalized him with all my demands." He turned to Charlie. "We couldn't have beaten the Hun without ground crew like Elizabeth here. She's been with the house since my mother was a girl."

"Go on with you. Just ring when you're ready. I'll serve in the small dining room."

Charlie followed him up the stairs. Withycombe opened a door in the paneling on a small bedroom.

"This is your room." He nodded to the single bed just under the window, a tiny wardrobe and a desk with a typewriter already on it. "You can decide what you want to do with that one. It's the one I always keep for my secretaries and so far, I think it's typed one letter."

Charlie saw that Robert had dropped his bag off in the middle of the bed. "This is fine, sir."

Withycombe opened a door in the wall by his washstand revealed a much larger bedroom. "And my room is just through here. You have a bell pull for the servants and I'm right here if you need me."

Charlie was very sure Edward didn't mean that to sound like an invitation. "Thank you, my lord." He'd meant to sound professional, and not meant to put that level of possessiveness into the title. Rather than embarrass himself more, Charlie started unpacking.

"We'll spend two days here, then on to London. You'll need formal wear for that evening. We can store it at the townhouse."

Withycombe settled into the chair before the typewriter, as Charlie tried to focus on putting his clothes away. "So, tell me about your family."

Charlie hung a suit in the wardrobe. "I'm a middle child. My brother's older, so he got a partnership in the family business. Mom and Dad are still living in Jersey. I had to go to school."

"What's the family business?" He pecked idly at a couple of typewriter keys, not hitting them hard enough to mark the paper.

"Dad's a tailor. Does really nice work, too."

"Merchant family. I think you've done better, getting your education." He rose and paused in the door. "We'll eat as soon as I change."

Charlie looked at the closed door for a little too long and then washed up for dinner himself.

*****

The next day, Withycombe took Charlie all over the enormous house, from attic to cellar, and the grounds. "Since you're going to live here, you need to know your way around."

Charlie had already found the water closets, retrofitted into the old house. They were functional, but not luxurious. The upstairs hall held bedrooms, sparsely furnished with heavy antiques.

Downstairs, he saw the formal dining room, where a hundred people could comfortably sit to a meal. They had eaten breakfast in the little morning room, a sun-drenched place with ceiling-high French windows. Charlie liked that one. Much of the house was dark and musty, clean but empty.

Afterward, they went to his library, a dim room, smelling of leather and wood, shot with the spicy scent of paper and the hint ghost of pipe tobacco. Charlie looked over a few titles and knew at once he would be spending many rainy afternoons and winter evenings before a nice fire in the hearth, reading in one of the big armchairs by the light of the fancy little lamp.

Withycombe rolled a cigarette as Charlie pulled the heavy drapes open to give the room more light. "Most of the books came with the house. One section is my father's that he moved here. I still have no idea everything we have in here." He lit the cigarette.

Charlie ran his hand lovingly over a shelf of books. "I'll catalogue them for you, if you'd like, sir."

Withycombe looked around, seeing hundreds of volumes. "That'll take some time. But it'd be very useful. There will be plenty of quiet afternoons to work at it." He beckoned Charlie onward.

The study was clearly his favorite room. The well-worn horsehair sofa and the faded rug attested to frequent use. It also smelled strongly of pipe smoke and Charlie saw several racks of pipes. A stuffed fox, only slightly moth-eaten, sat beside the fireplace like a faithful dog.

"My first hunt," Withycombe said, patting the fox behind the ears. A small bald spot in that location, clearly made by years of such pats, amused Charlie. "I got him when I was twelve."

Charlie looked around the room trying to learn more of his employer. Several decanters stood full on the occasional table, with glasses beside them. *A Study in Scarlet* had a bookmark about halfway through it where it lay on the end table near the sofa. Three kinds of tobacco, very different colors, all stood in their glass jars on a shelf.

Withycombe finished his cigarette and filled a pipe, settling himself in the armchair as Charlie roamed the room. Charlie sat on the sofa and opened the drawer of the end table, looking for matches to offer him a light.

A stack of naughty postcards made him forget his search immediately. He just stared for a moment, and then he shut the drawer and glanced up at his employer. "I can't seem to find the matches, sir," he said softly.

The smug smile said he knew exactly what Charlie had found. "You can have a look at those if you like. There might be a deck of playing cards, too. I do hope you're a good hand at Whist."

Charlie stood up. He saw the matches on the mantel and offered them to Edward. "I've never played. I'm willing to learn. But right now, I think I'd rather see the rest of the house." He knew, though, that he'd be back down to look at a later time.

"Any time you like. You know where they are." He re-lit his pipe and they continued the tour.

Charlie felt more comfortable outside in the sweet April morning. The birds twittered in the old orchard, just coming into bloom, and the shade was almost chilly as they walked out to the barn. A joyous baying sounded as they rounded the building and a pack of foxhounds leaped against the kennel railing.

Robert, the driver, came out, berating them in a cheerful sort of tone. "Down, you lot. Da will have something good for you. Behave, you."

Withycombe pressed against the fence, patting heads and getting snuffly doggy kisses all over his knees and hands. He called each hound by name and petted it. "My dogs. And you know Robert, who looks after them, among other things."

"Can't let them out, my lord. They're too pleased to have you back. They'd have you in the mud and lick you to death in a trice."

"Good lad. How're the horses?"

"In fine fettle. I was going to turn them out for a run after I fed this mob." Robert lifted a bucket of food.

"Let me know when you're ready. Think I might help out." He glanced at Charlie. "Do you ride, Charles?"

"Like a sack of potatoes in a rocking chair, according to my grandmother. But I can generally avoid falling off a horse."

"Then come see my darlings." The stable that smelled of hay and horse and sweet feed. "Who knows? You might like an English saddle better if you're used to those American ones."

Two fine horses stood in the stalls. A bay stallion whickered and Withycombe patted his nose with genuine affection. A chestnut mare stood in the next stall. Charlie offered to pat her as she nosed out for attention. She sniffed him and allowed him to touch her.

"Oscar is my boy. I've had him for ten years now, since he was a foal." He stroked the mare's nose. "Jamila, sweet, is Robert taking care of you right?" He turned to Charlie. "Most people won't ride a stallion, so I keep Jamila. She's very mild, especially gentle with lady riders. She might even tolerate a secretary who rides like a sack of potatoes."

Charlie managed a nervous grin. He hadn't been on a horse in five years. He didn't plan to start today. He watched his employer take the stallion's halter and open the stall door. Torn with indecision, he set his teeth and asked, "Do I need to get Jamila, sir?"

"Only if you want to. I'm just taking this boy out for a quick ride. I've missed him." He led Oscar out into the April sunshine and grasped his black mane. Charlie watched as he swung up, bareback, and offered a hand down. "You can come along if you like."

Charlie smiled. "No, thank you, sir. If you don't mind, I think I'll head back to the house."

"Suit yourself. I'll see you a little later." Withycombe nudged Oscar with his heels and they cantered off into the orchard. Charlie picked his way glanced back toward the house, determined not to go to the study. The last thing he needed was more stimulation.

He stepped back into the stables for a moment. Robert had finished with the dogs and was currying Jamila. Charlie leaned against a post.

"Need any help?"

"Not from a Yank who rides like a sack of potatoes." Robert gave him a grin to show he was teasing. "Just be a bit of company, if you don't mind, Mr. Doyle."

"Charlie, please. I'm not old enough to be Mr. Doyle."

"All right then. So how are you liking England?" Robert took the comb to the mare's mane. Charlie petted her nose.

"Very nice, so far. Is your lord always so…" Charlie waved his hand helplessly, at a loss for words for the first time in his life. "So overwhelming?" he finally said.

Robert laughed. "Oh yes. His lordship always has been, from the first day I saw him at the Harlow station. He'd just come home from the War, you see, to become Lord Withycombe. Even mourning his mother, as he was, he still nearly shone with vitality."

Charlie listened, rapt. "Being Lord Withycombe agrees with him. Servants, horses, all the wealth. Back home, nobody lives like this."

Robert shook his head. "Keep your eyes open, Charlie. We look good, because it wouldn't do for a baron to turn out poorly. There's a trust that handles the house and the servants. The horses and dogs, even the car, are required to maintain standing in society. But…" he He turned away, looking frightened of being disloyal.

"But what?" Charlie asked.

"Money flows through his lordship's fingers like water. He gets an allowance from his banker at the first of every month. Remind him on that day that he is to pay you first. You're not an actual part of the staff. He has no head for money. You may have to take that over completely. Other secretaries have." Robert hastily ducked away to fork hay down to the horses.

Charlie headed back for the house. Many things all made sense now, including the second class accommodations and the train ride when a baron could have hired a car. He took in more details on the way. The flowerbeds were raked over and danced blue with blooming iris. Only iris bloomed, which he knew was a perennial. No merry little pansies or petunias nodded among the tall, stately flowers. Once inside, Charlie strolled a little, snooping in the guise of learning his new home. The house was spotless, yet all the furnishings were antiques. The lights and plumbing all predated the War.

He settled in with his journal, keeping one eye out the window for his employer's return from his ride. He hoped they might do a bit more on the biography.

*****

The manor house almost echoed in its emptiness. It had been built in an era when lords lived in state with their extended families and many servants. A lone scion rattled around like the last bean in a can, even with his small staff.

Charlie liked the place, all atmosphere and gloom. He was somewhat surprised that his employer was in and out of his room a dozen times a day. He was used to being together all the time from the voyage across, but had assumed they would see less of each other with the separate rooms and Withycombe's duties.

He liked to sprawl on Charlie's narrow bed as Charlie typed. Charlie had moved his own typewriter onto the stand. Withycombe would lie on the bed and smoke his pipe and lie some more.

"The old place is haunted," he assured Charlie, on a rainy afternoon when the building creaked and groaned around them. "There's a suit of armor in the hall that rattles regularly." He gave Charlie a grin. "Since the manor house was not originally my family's, he's not an ancestor. It would be a splendid mystery to solve."

"I don't believe in ghosts, sir." Charlie adjusted his glasses. "You probably have mice."

"For shame, Charles. All your schooling has taught you to see no farther than the end of your nose. I thought you signed on to see the world." When Charlie nodded, he continued. "Not all places are so new as America. There are many strange things in many strange corners. Now, about ghosts, I don't believe in them, myself. You don't have to believe in something you've seen and know is real."

Charlie cracked his knuckles and prepared to take down another wild adventure. He loved it when he got the good stories. He typed away as Withycombe recounted the tale of a haunted French church, a spectral knight, and their regimental chaplain saying a midnight requiem under cold November stars. Charlie shuddered at the end of the story, not half-believing it but a shiver running over him anyway.

"Wow." He looked over to where Withycombe was relighting his pipe. "You've had some swell adventures. I can't wait for this one."

He sighed. "Let's hope we're on our way soon. I'll drive us into London tomorrow and we'll get you fitted out for the dinner party. I expect you to behave with all the manners your upbringing can muster."

"Yes, sir. I won't embarrass you."

Withycombe got up. Charlie shivered as one big hand came down on his shoulder. "I know you won't, Charles. Now, get us packed properly, please. With adequate clothing for any eventually. We may not have time to come back here to Harlow. We leave for London early."

*****

Charlie was much more attentive to the ride into London than he had been to the trip out to the manor. He watched as the little country houses grew taller and closer together and the broad lane narrowed to a city street. His employer was so good behind the wheel that Charlie wondered why he kept a driver.

He asked and Withycombe shrugged. "My father hired the lad. He handles so many things that I would have to hire three people to replace him."

Charlie endured the trip to the tailor, where he was measured in every possible dimension and then pronounced so ordinary that he could be fitted from stock. He'd known that. His father had often used him as a hemming mannequin. He was relieved when they reached the townhouse, a quiet building tucked into a less-fashionable area of the city.

Withycombe opened the door and Charlie recoiled from the stalking jaguar that appeared ready to strike. He breathed a little easier when he saw the beast was stuffed and made to appear to be lying in wait for any visitors. A tiger skin rug in the study hung him up, as did the lion that reclined by the study chair like a lapdog.

Lest his discomfort trouble his employer, he apologized. "I'm sorry, sir. I don't pretend to understand the pleasures of an outdoorsman such as yourself."

"It's just the thrill. And they are beautiful animals."

Rattled by the trophies, he followed Withycombe upstairs to the bedrooms. No servants attended them here, yet. Charlie aired out his room and hung up his formal dress. The evening loomed ahead like a very large test and he wanted to do his best not to make his employer regret hiring him.

"Charles, I can't find my cufflinks." Withycombe's voice was loud in the silence of the house.

Charlie put down his journal and got up. His employer Edward was the worst man for losing small objects that he'd ever encountered. In the country, he'd been called on a dozen times a day to find a lost pipe, missing jewelry, or a pen that had strayed.

He went into the master bedroom. Withycombe stood shirtless by the window, the sunset painting his strong chest red and gold, winking off a silver ring in his nipple. Charlie stared for a second, captivated by the man and wondering about that odd bit of metal, then went to the carpetbag.

"Your cufflinks are in the small velvet box with the rest of your jewelry. Your shirt studs are in there, too." He dug into the carpetbag, trying to ignore the handsome, half-naked man. He sensed more than heard Withycombe come up beside him. The big hand that settled on his arm drew his attention from the carpetbag. He looked up, holding the little velvet box in his hand.

Charlie felt his face soften, his lips parting as if for a kiss. His eyes widened a little and he tried to smile.

Withycombe took the box from his hand, his touch as deft as a pickpocket's. "Forgive me for being absentminded sometimes." He leaned toward Charlie's mouth as if to take the proffered kiss.

Charlie realized how he looked and straightened up. He cleared his throat. "Yes, of course. What am I for if not to remember all you've forgotten, sir?"

"Of course." The man's smile was gentle and Charlie wondered if he had misinterpreted the moment. He patted Charlie's arm. "Thank you. The maid and cook will be here tomorrow. Be ready in half an hour." As Charlie turned to go, Withycombe added, "If you need anything, you know where I am."

"Yes, sir." Charlie sketched a short bow. "I'm at your disposal. I'll be ready."

*****

The evening's affair was very formal. The personal secretaries and maids ate in a separate, smaller dining room from the guests. Charlie found himself wedged between a glum Irish girl and a cheerful blonde lady whose accent was so thick he had to ask her to repeat everything.

A slim blond man of about thirty sat catty-corner to him and watched him intently, an inscrutable look on his narrow, angular face. When the ladies retired from the main party, the maids did as well. The secretaries slipped in to lurk around the edges of the men's affair.

Charlie watched his employer, who looked very bored, drifting from one group of wealthy old men to another. Withycombe caught him watching and managed to meet him near the sherry and brandy. Charlie was sipping at some tea, mainly for something to do, and listening to the incomprehensible conversations.

"I'll get us out as quickly as possible, Charles. I have some prospects in line. Thank you for being patient." He took a glass of brandy and made his way back into the crowd with a smile stretched across his face.

"So," said the slim blond man, gesturing after Withycombe with his glass of sherry, "you're Lord Withycombe's new secretary?" A nasty smile crossed his high-cheekboned face. "Or is it catamite?

Charlie turned red and almost dropped his teacup when he realized the man was still looking at his employer and not him. "I beg your pardon?" Charlie asked as coldly as he could manage. His head spun at the suggestion that Withycombe could possibly be interested in him. Still there had been the moment with the cufflinks and a dozen other small instances. But surely not. He tried to keep his inclinations as private as he could, and the thought that a random stranger could see through him so easily was both startling and terrifying.

The blond man finally looked at him and extended a hand. "Nigel Drake. Secretary to Lady Sarah Brown, Edward's estranged fiancée."

Charlie set the teacup down after his hand made it rattle against the saucer again. At the rate this conversation was going, he was going to spill it or break it. He calmed himself by cataloguing Mr. Drake. The man was about the same age as his employer, and a few years older than him. No taller than Charlie, slim well-kept hands and a face Charlie was certain he had seen before. "Pleased to meet you. I'm Charlie Doyle." He tried to shake but Nigel pulled back and looked at Charlie's hand as if it were a week-dead mackerel, despite having offered first.

"American, I see." He made the word sound like a curse. Nigel sipped his sherry. "Well, do take care of yourself, Charles. It would be quite a pity for you to end up like the last one."

Before Charlie could ask what had happened to the last one, he saw Withycombe beckoning him. "Excuse me, please." He felt Nigel's eyes on his back all the way over.

He made his way over to where Edward—Lord Withycombe, he corrected himself mentally——waited. "Yes, sir?"

"We have a private meeting. Come."

Charlie, the word "catamite" still ringing in his ears, followed, his stomach sinking into his shoes. He was now quite sorry he had left his teacup sitting on the table. He could have used it to settle his stomach.

In a small drawing room, Withycombe made himself comfortable in a wingback chair. Charlie found a secretary's chair at his side, complete with writing equipment. He looked up from the pens when the door opened. A tall woman wearing khaki trousers, a cotton shirt, and a bush jacket strode in, followed by a mountainous bodyguard and Nigel. The formidable Lady Sarah, Charlie guessed, accompanied by her secretary. She swept across the room, kissed Withycombe's cheek before he could stop her, and settled herself on the horsehair divan. Nigel surprised Charlie by making himself comfortable on the floor at her feet and the bodyguard loomed behind her.

"How very unpleasant," Withycombe mumbled back to Charlie. "How did we get into this?"

A short man with an unfashionable walrus mustache and a monocle came in and looked at them. "Good evening. Thank you for joining me here. I trust you are enjoying yourselves. Brandy?"

Lady Sarah accepted a small glass, as did Nigel. The bodyguard refused. Charlie, wishing to keep his wits about him, said, "No, thank you."

Withycombe took a rather large glass. "Thank you, Sir Quincy. What do you have for me?" Charlie saw a frown-line between Lady Sarah's eyes at the singular.

"Very good, very good." Sir Quincy poured himself a snifter and settled into a chair before the fire. "As you may or may not have heard, Sir Alexander Spencer has gone missing in Egypt while exploring near the Valley of the Kings. This will not do. Already, the expedition is running into the tens of thousands of pounds and rumors of a curse or other trouble will start those superstitious natives to rumbling. That means trouble." He looked sharply at them. "That's why you're here, Withycombe. You and Miss Brown will find our missing digger. The one who brings him back gets rewarded."

"So why the competition?" asked Withycombe. "Why not simply hire one of us outright?"

Their host waved one soft, pale hand. "It's not a competition, exactly, dear boy. You are being hired by the university. Lady Sarah is in the employ of the Spencers. I thought it easier to meet with you both at once."

"Why on earth would they hire her?" Withycombe scoffed, and Lady Sarah gave him a sour smile. Charlie had to admit she was lovely, all milky skin and dark hair braided up atop her head, but her smile was purely predatory.

"Darling Ed, didn't your mother tell you that the most expensive isn't always the best?"

"Yes, but she also told me that quality doesn't come cheaply, Miss Brown." Charlie noticed no one used an honorific for the woman, which puzzled him.

Lady Sarah frowned. "Catty, Edward love. Very catty."

"Says the panther herself. I'm not here for you to strop your claws, miss."

Charlie watched this byplay closely,  taking mental notes. When their host began discussing the details of Egypt and the lost archaeologist, he pulled out the notepad he carried in his pocket and started making physical notes. He couldn't follow the discussion, but listed everything that sounded like a name or a date and hoped Edward could explain it. It all sounded very exciting. Egypt was where all the adventures were happening these days.

As they negotiated timetables and payment, Charlie kept very careful notes. It sounded as if they were to leave immediately. He saw Nigel doing the same in rapid shorthand.

Their host bade his farewells, bowing to Withycombe and kissing Lady Sarah's hand. Lady Sarah looked at them and smiled.

"I'll see you in Cairo then, my love." She rose and closed for a kiss.

This time he was ready and blocked her. She favored him with a smile that made Charlie shiver. Cold and challenging as her ice-white skin, Charlie suspected it meant she would devour them both if given a chance.

Lady Sarah made her exit and contented herself with blowing Edward a kiss from the doorframe. Nigel, trailing in her wake, did the same, but less extravagantly and with extra mockery.

Withycombe rose and poured two brandies, then flung open the doors to the balcony, letting in the night air. He offered one glass to Charlie, who stared for a moment. Charlie reached up and took the glass, letting his fingers barely brush his employer's. He was terrible at flirting, but, if Nigel was correct, he'd been chosen for more than his typing skills.

Withycombe looked down at him for a moment and Charlie felt his face tipping up for a kiss again. Withycombe shook himself and went to stand at the balcony rail, glaring down into the courtyard.

Charlie joined him there, flustered by the meeting. He watched Lady Sarah and her men climb into a Rolls Royce Cabriolet. He was still confused enough that he took a too-large swallow of the brandy, which made him sputter and cough.

Withycombe clapped him on the back. "It looks like we're going to Egypt to find this Sir Alexander Spencer fellow. Make no error, Charles, we will be the ones to find him."

They watched in silence for a few minutes. Charlie finished the brandy and felt a warm glow spread through him.

Withycombe smiled down fondly, or so it seemed to Charlie. "Time to go, I think." Charlie followed him out into the main room as he made his good-byes to the guests and their host. As much as he wanted to, he didn't hang on the man's arm, but simply stood at his elbow. The others ignored him.

To his surprise, Withycombe took his elbow as they started down the front steps to the car. He leaned into that. Nigel, for all that he was the enemy, had indeed been right. He scooted close for the drive home, but didn't lay his head on Withycombe's shoulder, knowing he needed to be able to change gears.

Withycombe relaxed and drove through the city. "That was better than I expected, even if we did have Miss Brown to handle."

"I had a nice time, sir," Charlie said, smiling.

"Sir Quincy usually gives terrible parties. I think he got a new cook. And his taste in friends has improved a bit too."

Charlie giggled and hiccupped a little when the car hit a bump. He was quite content where he was. "I am… drunk," he managed and, quite of its own accord, his head landed on Withycombe's shoulder.

"You are indeed. On a single brandy." He ruffled Charlie's short brown hair and tipped him back upright. "Americans."

Charlie giggled a little. "I never have been really drunk." The absinthe with Frank had been barely two mouthfuls and he hadn't been more than tipsy.

Withycombe's hand hadn't moved from his hair and traced his ear. "Do you like it?"

Charlie rubbed his cheek against the very warm wrist. "I'm not sure. I feel terribly silly, as if the world's not quite real. Or as if I'm not quite real."

His employer never stopped touching him. "Well, you won't feel so silly tomorrow. I'll make sure my Molly doesn't go knocking on your door too early."

Charlie sighed softly. "Thank you, sir."

"I think you should call me Edward." The hand in his hair traced down to his neck. Charlie settled in, making himself more comfortable on Edward's shoulder. They rode the rest of the short distance to the townhouse and Edward parked the car.

Neither man moved for a few moments, and then Edward tipped Charlie's face up to him. "Is this real?" he asked. He kissed Charlie, his lips soft and warm, moving very gently.

Charlie nodded as Edward let him up. "Very real." He stretched up, trying to get closer to Edward's lips. "The only real thing in the world."

He finally reached Edward's mouth and tasted it. More soothing than the tea, more warming than the brandy, Edward tasted of both these and of the tobacco and of himself. Charlie flicked his tongue over Edward's lips, trying for more of his taste and Edward opened to him. The warm wetness of his mouth encouraged Charlie and he plunged deep, taking what he now realized he'd wanted since the first day he'd seen Edward. It might never be more than this one moment, but he would have all he desired in it.

Charlie was dimly aware of big hands on the side of his face, holding him close. He became more aware as they eased him away, breaking the kiss.

"It's late, Charles. And you are going to have a sore head tomorrow." He kissed Charlie's forehead. "Up to bed with you. I've already taken shameless advantage of your first intoxication."

Charlie managed the steps, mostly by holding onto the rail with one hand and Edward with the other. They seemed to be a million miles away or right under his nose, sometimes at the same time. He made it to his room, shed his jacket, and vaguely remembered Edward undoing his tie. He wasn't sure if there was another kiss or not. He tumbled onto his bed, half-hoping Edward would follow, but was asleep before he could figure out exactly how to get off his shirt.

*****

Charlie awoke the next morning with a headache. The rain dribbling down the gray windowpane only put him in a worse mood. He rolled over and tried to go back to sleep. Maybe the rain and the headache would both go away. It was no good. He felt all wrong. He finally opened one eye and raised an eyebrow. He knew he hadn't taken his shirt or trousers off, yet he was in Edward's nightshirt and his formal-wear had all been hung neatly away.

As he turned over again, trying to get comfortable now that he had figured figured things out, his hand caught the bell pull. Now he'd done it. Maybe if he was asleep, the maid would leave him alone. He supposed the maid had arrived. There was a faint but distinct smell of cooking that made his stomach wobble a little.

A tap at his door a few minutes later heralded a pretty dark-haired girl with a breakfast tray, one containing a large pot of strong black coffee. The smell woke Charlie up completely.

"Good morning, Mr. Doyle. I'm Molly. The master said to bring this up as soon as you woke."

A vile concoction in a glass made him recoil from the food tray. "What is that?"

She handed him a note. Edward's appalling handwriting informed Charlie that there was a hangover cure and strong coffee if he needed them, and that Molly would see to anything else he required. Edward was out, discussing the job with their sponsor and preparing the plane.

Charlie drank the coffee and ate the porridge she'd brought up, leaving the kippers alone. He didn't need the hangover cure. It was just a little headache. He felt better after breakfast and got up and dressed. He could get used to breakfast in bed.

As he settled into the big comfortable chair to write in his journal, he found himself at a loss as to how to describe the previous night. He recorded the dinner party and Nigel and Lady Sarah, but then had come the balcony and the brandy and the car.

Oh, the car! His mouth tingled at the memory and the phantom hands held his head again as he remembered the kiss. Charlie shook himself and put his journal aside. He was not about to record that kiss in all the detail he could remember. Instead, he made a small "K" in the margin of the journal and went to his typewriter, hoping to clack the keys until the memory's heat had cooled.

He was still at the machine when Edward came in a couple hours later, looking very cheerful.

"I managed to prise a bit of travel money out of our skinflint employers," he announced. "Tight old prunes, you'd think every penny was being minted out of their hides."

Charlie stood up when Edward came in. "I must apologize, Edward," he hesitated and corrected himself, "sir, for my bad behavior last night and unprofessionalism this morning."

Edward grinned at him and ruffled a sheaf of banknotes under his nose, a most surprising development. Apparently money solved many mood problems for his employer. "That's perfectly fine, Charles. I'm fifty pounds to the good and in far too fine a humor to be put off."

Charlie boggled at the pile of cash, most of it in English pounds, some in large stacks of French francs. "And how much is that in real money?"

Edward laughed and flopped onto Charlie's bed, letting one leg dangle off the edge. Charlie swallowed hard at what looked like an invitation. "A lot. And there's two hundred and fifty more pounds coming once we deliver our lost adventurer." He winked at Charlie. "Plus, whatever else we find small enough to hide from the British Museum."

Charlie sat down and suddenly seemed to have too many elbows, because he wasn't sure where the one that clattered on his typewriter came from. Surely Edward wasn't suggesting tomb robbing. Stories from lurid dime novels about the wages of wrongdoing and Egyptian curses and vengeful ghosts rose up in his mind, only to be assuaged when Edward sat up.

"We depart Monday," he announced as he got up to leave.

Charlie nodded. "All right. I'll pack."

"Thank you, Charles." Edward stopped in the doorway and tilted his head. "I do hope you're not airsick."

Charlie straightened up in his chair. "We'll find out, won't we, sir?"

Edward nodded. "Brave lad. Yes, we will. A brief stop in Paris and then it's all train to the coast. I'm afraid you'll have to endure another ship across the Mediterranean. I hope you will be more comfortable."

"I like trains," Charlie assured him. He stood up, almost bouncing at the very idea of Paris. "How long will we have in Paris?"

"As long as I need." Edward looked at him, teasing. "You aren't planning to abscond with a can-can girl and spend the rest of your life living in a garret writing penny-dreadfuls, are you?"

"No, of course not, sir. Not with Egypt coming up, too!"

"Let me see about dinner. Maybe we can take in some sights before we leave London." He headed out and Charlie heard him whistling all the way down the stairs.

# Curse of the Pharoah's Manicurist

*****

The front bell interrupted their dinner and Charlie trailed Edward as he answered it. He gawked at the sight of Lady Sarah, fearless in khaki trousers, with an icy smile on her face. "I thought I should come say good-bye, darling. I'm off to Egypt."

Edward raised his eyebrows at her, his face full of cool disdain. "I do hope you don't get too angry when you lose."

She laughed, a brittle sound like ice shattering. "Darling Edward, you're always so amusing. You should know by now that I never lose."

He favored her with a nasty smile, one that made Charlie's blood run cold. "You lost me, didn't you?"

She patted his face, smirking when he flinched away from her touch. "Only briefly, my dear, only briefly. And that game is still afoot." Edward sighed and Lady Sarah stepped off the porch. "Since you haven't the courtesy to invite me in, I'll see you in Egypt, Edward." She swept off to the hansom that awaited her, the large bodyguard at the reins.

Edward looked very peeved as he shut the door.

Charlie hazarded a question to alleviate his confusion. "Edward? Who is Lady Sarah?" She baffled him and aroused him with her boldness. The pants were positively obscene on her.

"A woman who'll likely end up getting killed trying to prove a point." Edward sighed as he retreated to his half-eaten dinner. "Don't call her that, Charles. She's not aristocracy. She assumed the title and uses it, but has no right to it. You'll note, only her hirelings and those who are not society call her by it. Vulgar, really. Besides, the proper address is one's Christian name, one's surname, and then the title. If she bothered herself about anything but single-minded pursuit, she would know that." Edward sighed as he retreated to his half-eaten dinner.

"She looks more like she'd do the killing to make her point." Charlie brought up what had been worrying him. "She loves you, doesn't she?"

"She did once. We were engaged, long ago. Before the War." Memories twisted Edward's face. "Father said it was a good match, but we butted heads like rams in season. I never loved her."

"I think she loves herself enough for both of you," Charlie said and covered his mouth at his impertinence.

"Perhaps so. But no, she'll never give up. Not until one of us is dead." He sighed. "She can't win. We won't let her." Edward brought his fist down on the table, making the silverware jump and the oxtail soup slosh.

Charlie sat back down at the table, determined to help Edward in any way he could. "Perhaps we should leave today, sir? I took the liberty of remaining mostly packed."

"Good. So did I."

Charlie pushed away from his mostly empty plate. "Then let's go find out how airsick I get." He gave Edward a big grin.

# CHAPTER 3

# PARIS AND OTHER COMPLICATIONS

**Of** my first view of Paris, I would like to say it was magnificent. I was privileged enough to approach not from the north or south, but from above, as Lord Withycombe is a most accomplished pilot. I wish I could have seen the Cathedral of Notre Dame rising from its island in the middle of the Seine River and stared at the scarlet windmill of the Moulin Rouge in Montmarte, hypnotized by the spinning of its blades. Even thirty-three years later, the Eiffel Tower remains a marvel of modern architecture. But alas, we arrived by night. The City of Lights was exactly that, a glittering, spun-glass confection of lights that drew us down like insects trapped in the glistening walls of a pitcher plant.

—From the journal of Charles Doyle, secretary to Lord Withycombe

*****

Inside the cavernous hangar, tucked away on a back field of the Harlow estate, Charlie just looked at the planes. He recognized the much-lauded Sopwith Camel tucked toward the back and gaped at the bright red Fokker triplane.

Edward saw him staring. He nudged Charlie and handed him a flight-jacket and a leather helmet. "The Germans had to give us all their planes as war reparations. I had to have one. She handles like a dream." He ignored Robert bustling about, making sure everything was in order with the one they would be flying.

"Is it the Red Baron's plane, sir?" Charlie was still staring at an image out of one of his boyhood books that had come to life right in front of him.

"Oh, no. His was lost as far as I know." Edward brushed a bit of standing dust off the aircraft's nose. "I painted her in his style, though. It was quite the scandal a few years back. I took her up for a flight and no less than a dozen frantic calls came in to the constable about it." He chuckled. "And no, I never fought the baron himself. Saw him, once, but we didn't engage. Thankfully so, since I'd likely not be standing here talking to you right now if we had."

Charlie forcibly closed his mouth and looked down at the jacket and helmet he still held. "I feel a bit silly," he protested.

"It's very cold and loud up there. You'll want them both."

Charlie put them on, struggling with the helmet fastener. Edward suited with the speed of a man used to being jerked out of bed at a moment's notice. He fastened Charlie's helmet and snapped his own goggles into place.

They all three pushed the sturdy little DeHavilland DH-9 bomber out of the hangar. Robert chocked the wheels. "Ready when you are, my lord," he called.

"There we are, lad. You'll get used to this quicker than the ocean, I hope." Edward helped Charlie into the rear seat of the plane. "I bought this one, too, after the War. All the armaments are gone, so she's a lot lighter and faster now."

Charlie was only half-listening. He was too busy feeling Edward's hand on his rear, boosting him into the seat. He remembered to lower his goggles.

"Are you settled, Charles?"

"Yes, sir." Charlie couldn't keep the nervousness out of his voice.

Edward gave the plane a last last-minute check and climbed aboard himself. He told Robert to spin the propeller and he gunned the engine.

"Chocks away, Robert!" he called.

"Chocks away, my lord!" Robert called when he yanked the blocks out from under the wheels.

They taxied out, Charlie holding his breath. He relaxed as they went down the runway cut through the center of the oat field, picking up speed. Charlie gasped as the ground fell away, leaving only a fragile shell of wood and canvas between him and the rapidly dwindling earth. Robert, waving to them, quickly became a distant speck.

The wind rushed so fiercely he was glad of the goggles, but found it hard to catch his breath. Finally, he ducked below the level of the plane's dash just to breathe.

Edward glanced back. "Lovely weather, full moon," he shouted. "It should be a clear night all the way to Paris. It'll be about two hours."

Charlie stuck his head up in time to watch the sun set and the fat yellow moon rest on the horizon. "It is nice, sir." He ducked back down and pulled out his journal. The plane jostled so badly his handwriting was illegible. The darkness didn't help. He stayed down.

They flew for a while and then Edward shouted again. "We're over the Channel now, Charles. Great view."

Charlie popped back up and looked over the side, finding a way to breathe in the rush of the wind. He stared at the black water beneath them, the first stars reflected on it. "At least we're not sailing it!" he shouted back.

"Very true! You're not airsick, are you?"

"No, sir."

Charlie didn't see much of anything on the ground, once they made the French shore, just dark patches, with a few twinkling lights of farmhouses or towns and silvery shadows. The little plane seemed to float like a boat on a starry ocean, hanging in the sky and not moving. He recorded all this by the moonlight.

The lights on the ground grew closer together. Then a burst of brilliance shone out in the night. The spire of the Eiffel Tower jutted skyward, illuminated like a beacon. Edward flew them over it and Charlie stared. The headlights of cars creeping down the boulevards, the lit shop windows and houses, the monuments to battles fought before his own country had even existed, everywhere he looked there was something new to see.

"Best view you'll ever get of the grand lady Paree!" Edward called back.

Charlie just kept looking, storing it all, as they left the city behind. A string of lights on the ground grew larger and closer to them. The engine sounds lowered and Edward started bringing them down just south of the city.

Edward landed them with a jarring bump and rolled to a stop. He had Charlie help him push the plane into a barn, where a car waited for them. Charlie got the bags, while Edward started the car. He couldn't stop smiling as he loaded them and climbed in.

"Wow! That was really something, sir. All those lights, all the places I've only read about."

"She is beautiful, isn't she? Well, we have one night. We can't get drunk, but we can have some fun." Edward headed the car back into the city.

"Fun, sir? I'm not much for carousing. No more booze."

"Wine when in France. One glass of champagne can't hurt. And if you consider a single glass of brandy at Sir Quincy's dinner party carousing, we shall indeed have to broaden your experience."

Charlie sighed, remembering the brandy, and brightened a little at the thought of what had come afterward. "All right. But only one. I'm afraid I have very little head for it."

"Paris will be very good for you, then." Edward ruffled his hair as they came into the suburbs. "You'll love it."

Charlie stared at the people sitting in cafes and shopping, even after dark. "Will you dump me if I can't keep up with you?" Horrified that his fear had slipped out, he covered his mouth.

Edward gently pulled his hands down, then put both of his back on the wheel to avoid running over a cat that darted in front of them. "Of course not."

"I'm sorry, sir. My mouth ran away with me." Charlie felt his ears going hot. He had to learn to quit blushing.

Edward stopped the car, parking it along a side street. He put both hands on Charlie's shoulders and turned Charlie to face him. Charlie stared up, wondering if he was about to be kissed again. "I won't dump you. Full stop," he said earnestly. Then he smiled. "I'm very pleased with you so far. You're brave enough to step into completely unknown circumstances, taking work in a foreign country and traveling by new means. You work diligently and you are always ready for whatever wildness I propose next."

Charlie relaxed enough to laugh. "I've been seasick, dragged along, and absolutely useless to you, sir. Not to mention the fact I have the most abominable tendency to be improper."

"Nonsense. I like your company." Edward put the car in gear. "Very few people have the nerve to stand up to

Lord Withycombe, Flying Ace and War Hero. And fewer still are willing to fly with me."

Charlie could hear the self-mockery in the titles. He just smiled. They drove through the well-lit streets to Pigalle and the Moulin Rouge. Charlie had heard of the legendary cabaret, had seen Toulouse-Lautrec's paintings, and now his stomach turned flip-flops at the prospect of going into the famous building.

He didn't see how much Edward slipped the maîitre d', but they were shown to seats very close to the stage. Edward spoke rapid French, of which Charlie understood only every third word with his college French.

Just as the houselights dimmed, a girl in a frilly green dress delivered a rich pastry to him and poured out a glass of sparkling wine. Edward tucked a few bills into the neckline of her dress. She giggled and gushed at him in French. He tapped his cheek and the girl swooped down to kiss him.

Charlie just watched. He took a sip of the champagne to cover his nerves and the bubbles tickled his nose, making him snort a little. Edward turned and whispered to the girl. She kissed Charlie's cheek and cooed in his ear.

"*Américain?*"

"Uh, *oui*," he answered.

She giggled and kissed him again, then vanished in a swirl of flounces and lace to finish her rounds before the show began.

"They get prettier every spring," Edward said, pouring himself another glass.

Charlie nibbled at the pastry and watched, dumbfounded, as the riot of color and noise that was an authentic can-can took place not twenty feet from him. He felt as if he could reach out and touch the dancers, perhaps lose himself in the froth of petticoats and bright dresses.

Edward drank more champagne, called for another bottle and watched cheerfully. During a lull in the show, he reached over and touched Charlie's arm.

"Do you like Paris more than London?" Edward asked.

"It's… very different," Charlie said and poured a second glass of champagne. The pastry had been cloyingly sweet and although he wasn't at all certain he liked the fizzy wine, he needed something to wash it down. "London is better suited to my work."

"But Paris is far more fun. If we weren't leaving tomorrow, you could have taken a dancer home. Any of them are willing to go for the right price. You've been watching the little brunette in the red dress on the end. She might even like us both."

Charlie nodded, caught. After the kisses, was Edward really offering to buy him a woman? When the lights came back up and the dancers started circulating through the crowd, Edward beckoned the little brunette over to their table along with her taller blonde companion.

Charlie found himself all tongue-tied at the prospect of trying to talk to a girl in a different language. He knew he'd have been just as flustered in English. He watched Edward, who discreetly tucked a few bills into the girls' dresses. They nodded to each other and motioned the men to follow.

Charlie and Edward were reseated at a table in a private nook out of view of the stage. The blonde drew a curtain, then planted herself in Edward's lap and the brunette filled Charlie's with no hesitation.

He whispered a short snippet of poetry, which was all the French he could remember, and she giggled. The blonde was already kissing Edward. Charlie watched a moment too long and his girl squirmed on his lap, reminding him of the cuddlesome armful he had.

He stroked her face and kissed her. She wrapped strong, bare arms around his neck and promptly taught him why it was called French kissing. He moaned under her tongue and kept her there until he realized he had forgotten to breathe.

She released him and giggled as he gasped for air. He watched Edward kiss his girl and then noted that Edward was watching him. He smiled and kissed the girl again, remembering to breathe this time.

"*Bien, eh Americain?*"

"*Oui.*" He kissed her again. "*Mais oui. Merci.*"

"*Da rien.*" She tapped his nose and gave him a saucy smile. Then she reached for his fly.

Charlie set her on her feet, took a brief kiss of her cheek and stood up himself. "I'm sorry, I need the gentlemen's room. Excuse me, please." He headed hastily out of the alcove theater to cool off.

"Charles," Edward caught his arm as he left. "Be careful. I'll meet you at the front door in a few minutes."

"I will, sir." Charlie very carefully did not look at the girl in green or what she was doing. He didn't look at the girl in red, not wanting to see her hurt or puzzlement. He let himself out of the alcove and found his way out of the theater. Edward wasn't the only one enjoying himself. Every alcove had been open when they came in and now all of them were closed.

He strolled around the block and found himself back at the front door. He wasn't quite ready to face Edward and so did another turn, around two blocks, turning up his coat collar against the decidedly chilly April                                             night.
A man in a heavy opera cloak stopped him near an alley and asked the time in French. Charlie showed

his bare wrist, having forgotten the word for watch, and all of the lights in the City of Lights went out with a flash of pain in the back of his head.

*****

Charlie woke up, his head pounding like a marching band. The man in the opera cloak, who had asked him the time, sat on the edge of the bed, polishing his glasses, a pair of octagonal wire frames, unlike Charlie's round ones. Charlie groped for his own but did not find them. Even without his glasses, he now recognized the man as Lady Sarah's secretary, Nigel. Charlie hadn't much liked Nigel back in London, because of the man's nasty insinuations and sly manner.

"Good evening, Mr. Doyle. Please try sitting up." Now Nigel sounded coolly polite, not at all silly and flirtatious.

Charlie looked around, not bothering to ask where he was. It looked like a hotel room. He tried sitting up.

His stomach rebelled and his eyes crossed. He slumped back down, stopped only by the soft, lavender-scented pillows at his back. So much for the escape plan of punching Nigel in the face, and then running for it.

Nigel put on his glasses and looked across the bed. "I told you that you coshed him too hard." He ran very light fingers through Charlie's hair and found a large and tender bump behind Charlie's right ear.

"Sorry," came a low rumble from the bodyguard Charlie remembered from London.

"Try again, please, Mr. Doyle. Lady Sarah insists you walk in on your own feet." Nigel unfolded Charlie's glasses and set them on his face. The world came back into focus.

Charlie managed to sit up without losing the pastry he'd eaten, but the room spun for a minute. The two men sat on either side of him, making the bed shake and his stomach respond queasily.

They took his arms and stood up together, hoisting him to his feet, and half-dragged him to where Lady Sarah waited. She had been intimidating wearing trousers and tweed in London. Here in Paris, in a room of scarlet, wearing only black silk as she wrote, she set Charlie's head reeling more than the blow had. Her jet-black hair was down and long, and her pale skin almost gleamed in the gaslight. Her dark eyes bored into him before she turned back to the note, and he felt his knees weakening as he walked into the red room. Cherries, blood, bricks to dash his aching brains out, and her lips… ah, God, her lips, as scarlet as the velvet hangings. She looked like a vampire, and in that instant, Charlie knew she would eat him alive.

She looked up. "Nigel, dear, does this sound right?" She read the note she had just finished. "Darling Edward, I'm enjoying the company of your adorable young American. How typical of you to leave such a morsel unattended as you debauched yourself. Never fear, my dearest. He is perfectly safe. I will be keeping him with me to ensure your cooperation. Drop your chase now and no harm will come to him. Kisses."

Nigel smiled. "Perfect, my lady."

"Then Vincent, see that dear Edward gets this note, if you would?" She handed the large American the note and a small pouch of coins. He bowed out. "Ah, Charles." She smiled in a way that turned Charlie's blood to ice.

He steeled himself and walked toward her, with as much of a smile as he could manage, exactly as he imagined Edward would do in his place. She extended a hand and he bowed over it. The motion made his unstable head and stomach lurch sickeningly, and she drew back a bit. He knew he must look an unbecoming shade of green.

"Nigel, stay please. I may yet require you. I must apologize for my man's unseemly tactics. He is nothing but a crude American thug. He amuses me."

"Please, my lady, why am I here?" Charlie decided to err on the side of politeness and use the title she claimed.

"Because that, too, amuses me. Because you are Edward's. And it amuses me to take the things that are Edward's and make them mine. For he will be mine again shortly and what's mine will become his as well. So he gets you back in the end, after all."

Charlie's poor aching head spun with the twisted logic and he managed a semi-intelligible, "Uh, er..."

She put a hand in the middle of his chest and shoved him backward. He staggered two steps and dropped into a chair. She straddled his lap, much as the can-can girl had Edward, pinning him in the chair. Unlike the girl, who had been inviting and pliant, all Sarah projected was control. Charlie realized the fear was strictly his own.

He realized she was going to kiss him a bare instant before she did and once her lips were warm on his, there was nothing for it but to go along. He didn't dare bite her, but simply waited her out. From the corner of one eye, he saw Nigel smirk.

"I don't believe I shall need your assistance after all, Nigel dear. Please go guard the door. You may see to Vincent's needs when he returns. Charles and I," she stroked a long white hand over Charlie's face, "will be just fine."

"Call if you need us, my lady," Nigel said as he bowed out.

"Now, dear Charles, let us see what sort of taste Edward has developed these days."

Charlie shuddered and fought down the urge to dump her off and bolt for the door. He hadn't liked the look on Nigel's face, all steel-hard eyes and narrow lips. The jealous secretary would probably shoot him if he managed to get the door open. Instead, he tried to think what Edward would do in this situation. He had an idea but he doubted he could carry off reversing the seduction and escaping while she lay sated and sleeping. His inexperience was more likely to incapacitate her with laughter instead of exhausting her with desire and pleasure.

He struggled to get his arms free from where she had trapped them at his sides. She tightened her grip and kissed him again, more lingering this time, her tongue slick in his mouth, and when she let him go, she scowled.

"You're untouched." She sounded aghast. "Has Edward lost his desire for pretty boys already?"

Charlie couldn't bear the hope on her face. "No. I haven't been with him long. And I was seasick clear across from New York."

Sarah laughed. "So blunt."

"Yeah," he said and kissed the side of her neck. Maybe he could throw her off or something if he could shift them just a little. Her perfume was making his head spin.

She smiled at him. "Darling Charles, you really don't know a thing. I'd like to remedy that. Edward will certainly appreciate it."

"I'd rather you didn't."

She gave him the same carnivorous smile, and let a strap of her dress fall of her shoulder, exposing one pale breast. "Wouldn't you like to make your stay here more pleasant? I can make it very unpleasant if you cross me. And wouldn't you like to take some entertaining new ideas home to Edward when all of this is over?"

He saw her dangling the almost-promise of sending him home and was insulted. Surely she couldn't be planning to just hand him over at the end of this. He knew it was unlikely he would see Edward or England again. Vincent was more likely to bury his concussed, seasick corpse under a sand dune in Egypt, if they didn't just throw him overboard on the trip there.

The insult and impending death angered him enough that he quit being nice for a moment. He wrested one arm free and grabbed her by the shoulder. The slickness of the silk and softness of her skin did not stop him from shoving her away from him and gaining his feet.

Charlie felt his eyes unfocus, and the world went swimmy from the sudden standing. Distantly, he heard Sarah was yelling for Nigel to see to him. The ceiling spun like the windmill of the Moulin Rogue and Edward was there somewhere, laughing with one of the dancers. He had a vague memory of Nigel helping him back to the bed with the lavender-scented pillows.

Sarah's face surfaced amid the swirling grayness. "Well, I can see you'll be no entertainment at all. We leave for Egypt in the morning. There is no accounting for my husband's taste."

He sank into the lavender darkness, closed his eyes and dreamed he was back with Edward.

# CHAPTER 4

# CAIRO, CITY OF THE LIVING AND ALSO OF CARPETS

**Cairo,** city of the living, rises from the sands of Egypt, older than most Americans can comprehend. A thousand years old, it has withstood crusaders and sandstorms, Mamluks and Napoleon's troops. The Sphinx keeps a guard over it as the Nile, which bore both the Israelites and Cleopatra upon its waters, flows through the city.

—From the journal of Charles Doyle, secretary to Lord Withycombe

*****

Charlie stared out the porthole at the Cairo docks, four days later, watching the sailors and local men in their white robes, studying the bleached brick buildings and bales of goods. He wondered if he could fit through the porthole. He'd brave a swim in the Nile under the pilings and hunt for Edward himself when he was free. He took stock of what he had, for the dozenth time. His glasses, his wallet with ten dollars, mostly in change, his notebook and fountain pen. He was pleased he had left most of his pay in England, although robbery seemed an unlikely course for either Nigel or Vincent. He had nothing of use in an escape.

He looked up, jarred from his plans, when Vincent came into the cabin. Charlie had endured a miserable journey from Marseilles to Cairo. The seasickness of the Atlantic voyage had returned in spades and his cabin reeked of it, despite Nigel's constant cleaning. Lady Sarah had had nothing to do with him since Marseilles, so he counted himself lucky on that front.

"Up, you. She wants to see you." The big American folded his arms across his barrel chest and waited. Charlie took a quick look in the mirror, grabbed his glasses, and headed topside.

Lady Sarah waited on deck, attired in spotless khaki, a pith helmet covering her dark hair. "Charles, dear." She extended a languid hand for him to kiss. He just glared at her. "You're looking better. We're in Cairo. I'm sure you'll be happier on land, so Vincent is going to take you to my house. We'll be journeying on in a day or so. For now, we need you to recover so you don't slow the trip to find our missing Sir Alexander Spencer."

Charlie gave her a little bow but did not smile. "Your ladyship is most gracious. I'll be sure to have Edward express proper gratitude for the care you've taken."

Lady Sarah laughed. "You're picking up my husband's bad habits, including his acid tongue. Be good. If you give Vincent trouble, I can just as easily sling you over a camel. They stink so badly no one will notice if you're being sick."

Charlie gave Vincent no trouble as the big man led him through the hot dusty streets to a thick-walled stone house, built in the traditional flat-roofed style, not far from the river. The rooms seemed larger than those in England, but he suspected it was because they were mostly empty—only a few chairs here and there, a vase and a table, with none of the cluttered Victorian style of Edward's manor. He sat quietly when Vincent told him to, let the man tie him to a chair, and ignored the two men who bustled about, cleaning the place and airing the linens and mattresses.

When one clobbered Vincent over the head with a large vase, Charlie just watched the big man go down. He didn't scream or panic. The other man cut Charlie's ropes and said in accented English, "Lord Withycombe has some dictation you need to take."

Charlie stood up and rubbed his wrists. "Oh good."

The first man shook out a large carpet and gestured. The second nudged Charlie toward it. "We're smuggling you out in this."

Charlie understood and lay down on the rug, letting the men roll him up in it. It was just like the movies. Except the part where he couldn't breathe and was feeling much too jostled being carried. En route, he decided, half-suffocated and desperate to be on his own feet, that there had to be easier ways to travel.

When they set his rug down and unrolled it, Charlie got to his feet as quickly as the dizziness would allow. It wasn't a grand entrance, and he wondered how the legendary Queen of Sheba had managed to get her eyes to focus, let alone dance immediately after being unrolled. He wanted to hug Edward, who stood there smiling at him. After nearly a week in the company of Sarah and her men, with their informality, he found it difficult to think in terms of the man's title.

Instead, he gave a little bow and said, "I'm sorry I was so much trouble, sir. Apparently, it was a long way to the gentleman's room."

Edward laughed, and tipped the men who had delivered Charlie. When they left, he startled Charlie by seizing him into a bear hug, enveloping him in the smell of tobacco and warm skin. "I missed you dreadfully. And I think I lost my pipe this morning."

He held Charlie at arm's length. "So no more wrong way trips, is that quite understood?"

"Yes, sir. What did I miss, Edward, er, my lord?" Charlie fought the urge to melt back into Edward's arms and cling to him as if his lordship were a rock in a torrent. He wasn't blushing, for a change. Somewhere, he had lost that habit.

Edward let go of him with seeming reluctance. "Nothing but a ship and train ride. We won't be staying long. I have your bags with me. And yes, I think it should be Edward at this point, rather than all the formality."

Charlie nodded, surprised but pleased by the permission. He'd been thinking of his employer by name because Sarah and Nigel called him that. "I'm sure I stink. A bath and a change of clothes and I'll be ready."

Edward gestured into a bathroom. "Right in there. Nothing to be done about the water, I'm afraid. It will clean you well enough, but don't drink it."

Charlie nodded. After seeing the facilities, he didn't linger in the bath as he'd planned, but washed as quickly as he could and presented himself, considerably refreshed and much more pleasant smelling, before Edward in about half an hour.

"So, we're headed into the desert then?" He was ready for anything that came his way. He could endure anything after Lady Sarah. He didn't want to talk or think about her just yet. He was glad to be back with Edward, and everything else could wait until later.

"Oh yes. I stole one march on her and got here in time to set up your rescue. Now, we'll steal another. She'll want to refresh herself, and linger a day in her town house, to recover from the journey." Edward tossed him a full canteen.

Charlie took a drink and found it fresh and cool. He felt human again. He picked up a pack and slung a pair of saddlebags over his arm. "We shall have a day's advantage by starting now. I'm ready." Edward stared at him a moment. Then Charlie saw it. He dropped the saddlebags and grabbed the typewriter case. "You brought it!"

"The sand probably won't be good for it and we'll never be able to replace the ribbon in the desert, but yes, I brought it." Edward beamed as Charlie flipped open the case and ran his hands over the machine.

"Thank you." Charlie closed it up. He stepped a little closer and brushed a kiss over Edward's cheek, testing the waters, and his new knowledge of Edward gained from Sarah. "Thank you so much."

He went for another and was startled when Edward turned his head for a kiss on the lips. Charlie remembered the night in London and kissed him firmly, with no blushes and no hesitation.

Edward drew away a little, eyeing him. "Did Sarah show you a good time?"

Charlie shuddered and tried to avoid the question. "She's terrifying."

Edward nodded enthusiastically. "Yes, yes she is."

Charlie cleared his throat and figured it was best to tell everything up front. "I'm sorry, Lord Withycombe. I had no intention of poaching on your bride."

Edward sat down. "She won't get her hands on you again. But what on Earth did she tell you?"

Charlie took another drink of water. "She said you were to be married and that she was simply challenging you, making you prove yourself." He swallowed hard, but turned barely pink. "And… and that she wanted a taste of your latest Nancy-boy."

Edward scowled. "Put down your things. We aren't leaving right away. We're going to the bar. I need a drink and so do you. My erstwhile fiancée seems to forget a great many things. Including the small fact that our engagement was called off five years ago. And then we have an appointment."

Charlie followed him to the hotel bar, where he took the bright red cocktail that Edward ordered. He wasn't at all sure about drinking something called Red Death, but it went down smooth and sweet like fruit punch. "She said you liked boys... boys like me, better than any woman," he told Edward. "This was a test to see where you would go in reclaiming one."

Edward shrugged and drank his own Red Death. "Well, I have you back. What does that say to you?"

Charlie grinned at the thought of the rug. "It says you watch too many movies and have no idea how stuffy it is to be rolled up in a rug."

Edward laughed at that. "Finish your drink and then we'll be about our business. She'll be noticing you're gone very soon and I should like to be leaving by the time she finds us."

*****

They didn't leave Cairo at once. The first afternoon appointment was the Egyptian Museum. Sir Alexander had a working relationship with the curators, they learned from the assistant, giving them first choice of the artifacts.

Charlie pretended to examine an exhibit while Edward waited for the head curator. He stared at the wax cone, half-moon bronze razor, and cosmetic pots in the large case. "Tools of the Manicurists to the Pharaoh," the sign read. He moved on to a case with a tiny mummy in it. A large display told of Egyptian funerary rites and the preparation. A second display dealt in legend and superstition that had grown up around the dead.

As he waited for Edward, he lost himself reading the legend of how the powerful among the dead could send lesser minions back, disguised as humans, to destroy their enemies. These minions had but to touch a man and he would begin to wither and rot, becoming a mummy under the control of the more-powerful dead. The only cures for the mummy rot were—

"I am so sorry. Sir Alex has been in the Valley of the Kings for the last month." The curator's distress was hardly genuine as it interrupted Charlie's reading. Charlie lost his place and looked up.

Edward nodded. "We were hired by the British Museum to bring him home. A woman and man from the Spencer family are also on the hunt." He leaned in and smiled. Charlie saw him slide some folded bills to the curator. "We'd appreciate it if Sir Alex was expected to drop in tomorrow, whichever tomorrow it is for them."

The curator nodded. "Yes, yes, I think my good friend will cable me with regrets about a day after they come."

"Many thanks." Edward hustled Charlie out of the museum. Charlie caught glimpses of gold and other interesting objects, but there was no time to examine them.

"I've bought us another day," Edward explained as they hurried across town. "Maybe more."

*****

Charlie had expected camels, not a train, even so rickety a contraption as stood on the rails. The locomotive was a type that had long been replaced in America. He surmised it was held together with a glue made primarily of mud and sand. He followed Edward aboard that evening and was surprised when Edward immediately closed their tiny first-class compartment door and opened the dirt-dimmed window.

69

"Otherwise, we shall be mobbed and crowded, even here." Edward looked around. "The accommodations aren't much, but they'll do."

Charlie saw it was true. People even rode on the roof of the third-class cars. They'd be more comfortable than that at least. He made himself comfortable and took out his notebook. "Where are we going, Edward?"

"The Valley of the Kings, near Thebes. That was where Sir Alexander was lost. It's about four hundred miles. The railway is not yet complete, so we'll be taking camels the last fifty miles."

The train chugged and started pulling away from the platform. Edward smiled. "This is the only train on the track. It goes there and comes back. If Miss Brown misses it, she'll have to barge it upriver like Cleopatra. And four hundred miles is a long way to row." His smile broadened as he saw Nigel skid onto the platform just as the train left, trying to fight his way through the crowds of Egyptians. Charlie caught sight of the little man as they chuffed away. Nigel must have seen them for he tore his hat from his head and shouted something furious that was lost to the noise of the train.

"Make yourself comfortable, Charles. It's an overnight ride." He took out his pipe and settled in, smiling.

"You're in a good mood." Charlie jotted notes about his uncomfortable trip and his rescue by rug.

"They missed the train. Or, if Sarah made it, Nigel did not. Since he is more than half of the brains of the operation, they're delayed either way. She won't move without him. Perhaps he was just following us to report."

"Ah, good." Charlie felt an unpleasant smile spread itself over his face. He hadn't liked Nigel in London and he liked the man a good deal less here in Egypt after four days in his company aboard the ship.

"Very good, indeed."

Charlie rode a while, writing and watching the night fall in the desert. He sipped at the canteen and tried to ignore his hunger. He had a feeling they would be on short rations for a while, since they were traveling light, and that he would miss the rich pastries and even the good solid bubble-and-squeak the cook at the manor made.

"Charles, are you ready for a bite? Let's see what I can do about dinner."

"Is there a dining car?" Charlie tucked his notebook away and almost bounded to his feet.

Edward laughed, a hollow sound. "This is Egypt, my boy, not Britain or even America. We're lucky to have seats. The line isn't even finished past Thebes. I'll do a bit of a fry-up for us."

"Yes, please." Charlie's stomach rumbled loudly.

"This will be of the better-than-nothing school of army cooking, I fear." Edward set out a little charcoal burner and opened two cans with the attachment of his knife, setting them to heat atop it. "Bit of Maconochie and some bully beef." He opened a bag and pulled out a loaf of bread. "At least this is fresh from Cairo."

Charlie figured out that Maconochie was a canned vegetable stew and the bully beef was canned corned beef. It wasn't bad, just kind of bland. The bread was nicely chewy. He could handle eating like this for the trip. It would be better than dying of dysentery from whatever the locals in second class were cooking. The garlic and oil stench reached all the way up, despite the fresh air blowing through.

"That would be a grand way to make a fortune in a business. The man who could make this slop taste good would have the world beating a path to his door," Edward grumbled. "I do miss Paris."

"It's not bad," Charlie said. "Beats living on noodles and onions, as I did in school."

"Here." Edward scraped the last third of his food into the mess kit bowl Charlie held. "You probably need it more. If I know you, you haven't had a square meal since London." He lit up his pipe. "Tobacco is always cheap in Egypt, at least."

Charlie finished eating, feeling fuller than he had in a long time. He cleaned up the dishes and made sure the charcoal burner was out. The train rocked too much to open his typewriter, so he just noted their dinner and how nice it was to be back with Edward. He looked up a couple of times and caught Edward looking at him, studying his face, his hands, his very intent way of writing. He took out his notebooks and smiled.

"Ready for some more biography, sir?"

"Now does seem the time." Edward lit a second pipe and smiled. He dug a little in his bag. "There you are," he said to a small tin. "I knew I packed the pozzy."

"Pozzy?"

"Jam, Charles. Gooseberry jam." He spread a knife full of the pinkish glop over a hunk of bread and took a bite. "Mmm, much nicer." He offered the tin to Charlie, who got a small spoonful and put it on the end of his bread. The tart gooseberry taste made him wince.

"So, Edward, anything you'd like to tell me. School, the war, whatever. Or," Charlie closed the notebook and leaned forward, "tell me the tale of Nigel."

"Ah, yes, Nigel Drake, RFC. You got a chance to speak with him, I'm assuming?"

"Not much, sir. I wasn't really well enough." He listened, making notes on Nigel as he would a venomous snake.

"Nigel was in my squadron. Not a bad pilot, but he has a terrible temper. I had to ground him more than once for it. He resented discipline, as the educated merchants almost always do. They think it's for the lower classes and that they are too clever to be ordered about.

Alas, he was stunning in those days and had a taste for men to rival his need for flight."

"I got the wrong side of his temper, sir. He was really mad that I got seasick. I never heard a man swear so much."

"Yes, his fuse is short. He's a very dangerous man now, although you'd never think it to look at him. He despises me. I suspect he despises and resents you as well, for taking his place. After the war, I took him on as a secretary. We were knocked about Europe for a year or so but ultimately we proved," Edward thought a moment, visibly searching for the right word, "incompatible." He shook his head. "I suspect he's as mad as Sarah is. Many of us went a little mad in that hell. The ones that died weren't always the unlucky ones. But never forget, Charles, he is dangerous. Very dangerous. Highly intelligent. Never underestimate him."

"I won't, sir." Charlie had made all the notes he could. Edward stared out the window at the nighttime desert, his pipe gone cold.

"What else would you like to know about him?" The words sounded flat as if coming from a distance.

"Did you love him?" Charlie asked, little shocked at his own daring.

Edward gave Charlie a long, searching glance and smiled just a little. "Once," he said softly. "For a brief while."

Charlie set the notebook aside and went to sit on the padded bench next to Edward. Quietly, he said, "I'm sorry I ran out on you in Paris."

Edward ran a thumb down the side of Charlie's face. "You were wise to run. Even though the girls sell the service, the management makes a side bit on throwing out customers in disgrace and taking bribes to let them back in. We might have both been out on the pavement. And the bitch would have had us both. Then where would we be?"

Charlie smiled. "Certainly not here, in a first class train compartment. And doing this." He kissed Edward's cheek. Edward's long fingers tipped his face around. Charlie closed his eyes and Edward kissed him properly. His fine mouth moved gently and Charlie opened beneath it.

"We'll do more when there is true privacy," he said. "Even these kisses are still illegal. In Britain, I can be sentenced to prison. Here, we can be killed. Never forget that." He took another kiss. "Go to bed, Charles. You'll have everything you want, in due time." He settled back against the banquette.

Charlie nodded. "Soon."

Edward took a breath and sighed deeply, a pleased and contented sigh. "Oh yes," he agreed. "But sleep. There is a long day ahead tomorrow."

*****

The train arrived in the cool of the morning, but outfitting for the desert proved to take much longer. There was an interpreter to hire, gear to buy, water to draw, and camels to haggle for.

All the merchants wanted to haggle. The argument, with wild gestures and spitting insults, seemed to absorb them more than the sale. Edward, using an interpreter, was at a distinct disadvantage. Charlie listened closely and repeated phrases from the boy they'd paid to translate. He decided then he would learn Arabic as well as more French, so he could do the haggling next time.

Charlie discovered camels stank worse than he'd expected. The driver taught them basic commands. They loaded their meager baggage onto one kneeling beast, strapped a number of water bags that resembled dead goats to the other two, and prepared to mount.

For the first time since Charlie had seen him, Edward strapped on a revolver.

"Can you shoot, Charles?" he asked, sighting along the barrel before holstering it.

"No, sir. I'm sorry." Charlie was strictly a city boy. His cousins had taunted him about his inability to shoot or ride well or do much of anything more exciting than hoe weeds at his grandparents' farm when they'd spent summers there. He hadn't been able to see much past the end of his arm and it had made him a timid child. Now, he looked at the camels and decided he was making up for all of that.

"A deficiency in your education I shall have to remedy soon." Edward climbed aboard the camel, jerking its head to one side so it couldn't stand up on him, then making himself comfortable on the padded leather and wood saddle.

Charlie imitated him but found the saddle too broad to be comfortable. He shifted until he could sit easily. It was going to be a long ride, from the look of the water bags.

"Hut-hut," Edward ordered, tapping the camel with the small crop. It took three steps forward and then lay back down on the ground. Charlie's camel paused beside it. "Up, you flea-bitten beast," Edward ordered and struck it harder.

The camel turned its head back and spat, but it got up and walked out into the hot afternoon. Charlie's animal moved slowly, with a gentle rocking motion and followed it.

They rode until sunset, the Egyptian sun beating down on their hats. Charlie sweltered in the long-sleeved, light cotton shirt, but knew his skin would have broiled without it. When they paused at an oasis for supper, he was glad to slide off the camel. The motion was too reminiscent of a boat for the comfort of his stomach, yet not enough like one that he could be sick and get it over with.

They tied the camels to a palm tree and Edward, looking very flushed and overheated, stripped off his pith helmet and shirt. Charlie watched helplessly as Edward scooped up a helmet full of water from the well and poured it over himself. Charlie swallowed hard at the sight.

From all Nigel and Lady Sarah had said, and Edward's own behavior at the Moulin Rouge and on the train, there was no doubt left in Charlie's mind that Edward was as interested in men as he was in women, and Charlie in particular.

"Come cool off, Charles. Have a drink. You'll need it. We'll eat and move on. The next oasis is a night's hard riding. We'll spend the day there."

Cool off. As if he could cool anything in the presence of that sculpted torso that resembled Greek statuary, or that wide, laughing mouth that had kissed him so eagerly in London and on the train. Charlie walked toward the pond, seeing only Edward and the drops of water glistening on his body in the sunset.

He reached out to touch the ones that had collected on the silver ring and were just about to fall when a sheet of wet cotton intervened. Edward had wrung out his shirt with water and put it back on. Charlie blinked and got himself under control. The interest might be mutual but this was not the time or place. Edward's words about the illegality made him glance around, just to be sure they were alone.

Edward held him away at arm's length, looking at him. "Drink more," he said. "You're getting dehydrated already. And you look green again. Most unflattering. Is the camel a problem?"

Charlie cast about for his water-skin to cover his embarrassment. It was still on the camel. "Maybe a little, sir. It's kind of like a boat."

"They aren't called ships of the desert for nothing, Charles." He handed over his own waterskin. "Drink. Not a lot at first, but some. And sit down in the shade." He scooped a pith helmet full of water. "Do you want me to just pour or would you prefer to soak each piece of clothing? It will help cool you."

Charlie nodded. "Just pour please. I didn't know it could be so hot."

Edward smiled and poured the water gently over Charlie's head. It flowed cool and refreshing. He knew he'd be overheated soon enough, but this felt so nice he couldn't care. When the last had streamed down his back and stomach he opened his eyes.

"Thank you."

"To the shade, my boy. Drink and I'll make supper."

Edward poured some water into a bowl and added what looked like some strips of leather to it.

Charlie sipped at the water, feeling a little better for the shade. Edward unpacked his little charcoal burner and some charcoal and set about getting supper as night fell. "I should do that, sir," Charlie offered.

"You drink and rest. I'm used to this sort of thing. I don't want you collapsing on me tonight."

Charlie just watched him cook. Crouched over the charcoal burner, lit by moon and waning stars and red flames below, Edward looked dangerous and savage. Every now and then Charlie could see the dark splotch of the tattoo or the shine of the ring through his drying shirt.

Finally, knowing that if he drank any more water he'd float away, he found his voice. "Edward, may I ask a personal question?"

Edward looked up from the mess kit skillet, smiling, and Charlie caught the drifting scent of meat and potatoes and onion. "Certainly, Charles."

"Why do you have the ring there? And what is the tattoo? I never got a really good look."

"The tattoo is my regimental crest, a crowned cockatrice. Several of us got roaring drunk one night and went and got them. Nigel gave the others and me blue blazes the next morning, until I opened his own shirt." Edward's smile faded. He stood up and poured half of the potatoes into the bowl of the mess kit and handed it to Charlie. "The ring." He sighed. "After the war, I… well, Sarah and I had a brief rekindling. Very brief. She gave me the ring, since I enjoyed hers so much. She does still have them, doesn't she?"

It was Charlie's turn to hesitate as he opened the fork attachment on his utility knife. "Yes," he said in a very small voice. The bosom rings were just one more terrifying aspect of the whole frightening lady. He found the meat was some sort of dried, salted beef.

Edward touched it through his shirt. "I should get rid of it," Edward mused, before taking a bite of dinner. "But I like it."

"So do I," Charlie said and stuffed a bite of too-hot potatoes in his mouth to avoid saying anything else stupid.

Edward's smile returned. "I'm rather surprised I didn't find one or two in you when I had you kidnapped back."

Charlie swallowed very hard, the onion suddenly choking him. "She was going to do it that night in Cairo. She said she was going to lead me around by a leash in it, like a pet." His voice went soft on the last words. He told himself it was mostly fear and shame.

"Always best to heal a bit before you do that. Take it from the voice of experience." Edward shot him an impish smile and Charlie dropped the empty mess kit half and utility knife he held. For the first time since Lady Sarah had taken him, he knew he was blushing again.

The image of Edward shirtless, a leash in that ring, being led across the room by Lady Sarah struck him full force. Charlie busied himself recovering the utensils, taking much longer than he needed to, keeping his flaming face toward the sand until he cooled.

"If you'd like, I can pierce them for you. It does add the most amazing sensations to lovemaking. Not here, of course," he added as Charlie touched the neck of his own shirt, whether to hold it closed or open it he wasn't sure, "but in Paris." With a wink, he picked up the bowl and scrubbed the mess kit before packing it. "The can-can girls find it quite exotic."

Charlie went brighter red at that, and hid behind untying the water-skin. He refilled it while Edward doused the charcoal and watered the camels.

When he was still pretending to clean up and pack, Edward came over to him. Edward lifted Charlie's chin with one hand and looked at him, and Charlie saw the worry in his face that this time he'd teased too much. Charlie smiled up at him, finally recovered from his embarrassment. When Edward stroked a finger over his lips, almost a question, Charlie nodded. To his great pleasure, Edward's arms encircled him and held him close for a very long kiss.

One of the camels nosed at them, making them part with a laugh and Charlie turned to see it nibbling at the knots that held the pack camel, untying them with its prehensile lips.

"We need to keep moving." Edward tucked his own shirt back in and threw on a jacket against the nighttime chill. Charlie untied the other camels. As he prepared to climb aboard, Edward laid a hand alongside his face. "We will find time to take this wherever you wish it to go, Charles, love," Edward promised.

Then he wrestled his cantankerous brute of a camel to the ground so he could mount, leaving Charlie to dream of the kiss and the promise of more.

"Koosh," Charlie ordered, remembering his command lesson from the camel salesman. His own camel lay down quite placidly and waited for him to mount.

*****

They rode through the night, under the stars that looked big enough and close enough to touch. The half moon rose about midnight. Charlie found he could doze in the camel's saddle and not fall off. He never went completely to sleep and his memories of the night remained a blur of black sky, black sand, enormous stars, and Edward's voice, which filled his dozing with song and stories.

The tale of the goddess Nut, who stretched over the whole sky, her fingers and toes touching the cardinal points, filled Charlie's half- dreaming mind, followed by Isis and Osiris and how that lady made do when her husband was dismembered.

Once, music jolted him awake and he heard Edward singing, in a fine baritone, about the old cookhouse where all they got was pork and beans, which made the old soldiers fade away. Charlie tapped the camel and joined in when he moved on to "The Caissons Go Rolling Along."

"You sound good, sir."

Edward smiled at him and his teeth were white in the moonlight. "I'm trying to stay awake and find the oasis." He patted down his pockets. "Charles, I have the pipe and my tobacco…"

Charlie checked his own pockets. "Here, sir." He rode up beside Edward and passed the box of matches over. He'd become quite adept at anticipating Edward's needs and having the item to hand.

"Good lad."

"Do you know…" Charlie hesitated a little, "Do you know 'Roses of Picardy'? It's my favorite."

"I do." He lit the pipe and smoked a while. Charlie rode close, loving the smell of the smoke. He hadn't acquired a taste for the tobacco, but he enjoyed it when Edward smoked.

They rode for a while after the pipe went out and then Edward began in a sweet voice,

"She is watching by the poplars
Colinette with the sea blue eyes
She is watching and longing and waiting
Where the long white roadway lies."

Charlie hummed along, smiling. As the moon was setting, he saw a patch of trees on the horizon.

"Is that it, sir?"

Edward looked. "It is indeed. Perhaps you're not so blind as your glasses think."

They made for the oasis and reached it in the cold hour before dawn. Charlie tied the camels, using the most elaborate knots he could remember from Boy Scouts. He didn't want them untying themselves. Edward pitched a low sand-colored tent and spread bedrolls. "It will get hot, but we should have a nice updraft. Get some rest, Charles." As Charlie folded his glasses carefully and tucked them into his typewriter case, Edward pressed the box of matches into his hand. "Keep track of these for me, my dear."

He sipped water and scribbled in his journal as Edward lay down for the day. His boss was out as soon as his head hit the ground. Exhaustion from the eventful day and hard-riding night overcame Charlie, and he slept, too.

*****

Charlie awoke at sunset, sweaty and dusty, but feeling better. A light washing with a damp handkerchief and a couple of swallows of water had him up to snuff and happier than he'd been since Paris.

Lady Sarah had not cared much for his comfort, only for how much he amused her. When his usual *mal de mer* claimed him, she found him distinctly unamusing. Nigel had tended him indifferently, making sure only that he ate and stayed reasonably clean.

But now he was back with Edward, who by all accounts and actions was promising a very sweet lesson when they were someplace safe. His Edward, who had sung for him and who was now snoring. Charlie decided not to smother him with a pillow. He crept to Edward's side and just as Edward snored out, Charlie covered Edward's mouth with his. When Edward breathed in, he got a mouthful of Charlie's tongue instead of air. Edward was fully awake when Charlie stopped kissing him.

"We're well and truly private, sir," Charlie said, deftly slipping out of his shirt and trousers. He was a little worried. Edward felt oddly hot.

"Get dressed, Charles," he groaned. "As much as I appreciate your enthusiastic wake-up call, I am in no condition to enjoy your attentions." He sat up. Charlie saw he was sweating and shivering at the same time.

"My lord? What's wrong?"

"Malaria, Charles. I caught it in Africa a few years ago. Of all the deucedly inconvenient times for a flare up." He sank back to his bedroll. "Our two day advantage may be lost."

Charlie frowned. There were several options, none of them good. "I could stay and tend you. Or I can continue the search by talking to the other scientists working at the Valley of the Kings."

"No. I'm going with you. Just give me a moment to collect myself." He struggled to sit up.

Charlie pushed him back down on the bedroll. "You're doing nothing of the sort. You're too ill to sit up in your bed, let alone ride a camel all night. I'll ride down to the Valley and ask around."

"Take two camels and bring Dr. Jarvis Walker back with you. I checked in London and he is on this expedition. I need to consult with him. He knows Sir Alex better than anyone. Ride due south-east. You'll find it."

Charlie brought a canteen and one of the water-skins to the tent for Edward. He set the ration bag in easy reach. "You rest easy. I'll be back before morning with Dr. Walker."

"Says the man who gets his head bashed on the way to the loo."

"I just won't give any heavily-cloaked Frenchmen the time." Charlie grinned at him. Then, growing more serious, he kissed Edward. "I'll go fast and return quickly."

"Be careful, darling."

"Not only are you feverish, you're delirious." Charlie hugged him tightly. "I'll be all right. You just rest and try to get better. Is there any quinine in the bags?"

Edward shook his head. "I forgot." Even as ill as he was, he managed to sound sheepish.

Charlie jotted "Dr. Walker, quinine" in his notebook. "I'll see if they have any to spare." He stole a kiss and slipped out of the tent.

"Don't get lost," Edward called after him.

He had learned to saddle the camels when they got the beasts and now he saddled both, threw a water-skin and some food into a pack for himself, and started out. He kept an eye on the compass, the moon giving him enough light to see it.

The night was pleasant for riding, but he missed Edward. They were indeed moving quite fast on this romance, if that was what it was. Charlie wanted it to be a romance.

He wanted more kisses and whatever might come after them. He wanted to wake up next to Edward on a hundred mornings or late night expeditions. Thinking about these, he guided the camels into the Valley of the Kings. The night sentry demanded to know who came at such a late hour.

"Charlie Doyle, secretary to Edward Kilsby, Lord Withycombe. His lordship has been stricken with malaria and we require quinine and Dr. Jarvis Walker."

"I can't let you come in. We have typhus in the camp. Nobody enters or leaves."

"Then just give me the quinine and let me talk to the doctor!" Charlie barked. He didn't know where that particular bit of command had come from. But it seemed to rouse the man.

The sentry stirred at those words and sent his companion into the camp. Charlie made the camels kneel and climbed down.

Dr. Walker was a hale man of about sixty with a large nose and iron gray hair. He stood well away from Charlie, his nightshirt flapping in the desert breeze. "What's this about Eddie being ill?" he demanded.

"Malaria episode," Charlie said. "He forgot the quinine. And we need to talk about Sir Alexander Spencer. I brought camels and he needs to see you."

Dr. Walker chuckled a bit. "Oh, I see. The man would forget his head were it not attached. Let me get my clothes and the medico."

"I only brought one extra camel. I thought you were a doctor."

"Of Egyptology and Archaeology, and a couple of other things, but not of Medicine, lad." Dr. Walker vanished among the tents to dress. He came out accompanied by a tall ruddy man with a doctor's bag.

The sentry tried to stop them. "You don't want to spread the typhus."

"Nonsense. We'll stay on the sand and well away. Any lice we have will only bite us," the medico said.

They mounted the camel together and Charlie got on his. The medical doctor drove the animal hard. Charlie kept a close pace with the doctors.

"It's not far to our camp. Just a couple hours to the oasis."

"You're a good lad," Dr. Walker said. "And dear Eddie owes me yet again. He's run up quite a tab now. But I'll call it all settled if he finds Sir Alex. Feckless fool, rode back to Cairo alone. He's another of those who can't remember which way is north. Then once up there, he wandered out from the main dig at Saqqara."

They rode harder, pushing the camels well above the usual walk. The moon hung low when they reached the camp. Charlie tied the beasts while Dr. Walker and the medico, whose name Charlie still didn't know, hurried to the tent, staying outside of it. He heard a low groan from Edward and hurried the tying.

"Be good," he told the camels and ducked into the tent.

"Give this to him, lad." The medic handed Charlie a cup.

"Drink, my lord," Charlie, said. "It's the quinine."

Edward looked around and seemed to relax when he saw Charlie. "Yeargh. Those things grow more bitter every year," he said after the first gulp, his face pale in the lantern light. "Charles. They're poisoning me with army-issue quinine. Pack the good quality one from the druggist next time."

"Bosh, my lord," said the doctor.

"And, Davies, you old sawbones. You've been aching for a chance to work on me since France. Now you have me at your mercy. I trust I'll wake with all my parts intact."

"And here I was going to take a charitable contribution from your lordship's—ahem—privilege and aid the less well-endowed." Davies's face remained serious, but his blue eyes twinkled with mischief.

Despite his sickness, Edward chuckled. He beckoned Charlie over and wrapped his arms around him, pressing close for body heat against the chills. "My secretary will have words with you about that. Long words. Typewritten words, even." He held Charlie very tightly as the visitors laughed.

Dr. Davies excused himself and Dr. Walker got comfortable. Edward told him everything, from Sarah Brown and the competition to Charlie's two kidnappings, the first by Sarah, the second by his own men. Dr. Walker laughed at the tale of the rug and then grew serious.

"You shouldn't encourage her, dear boy. She's only doing it to keep your attention, which you give her, time after time. Ignore the poor deluded girl and she'll soon give up the insanity."

"She doesn't. She escalates it. And I won't be bested at my own game!"

"Easy, Edward, lad. Easy. You always were too competitive, and now look at you."

"I don't need your lecture. I need information about Sir Alex's disappearance," Edward grumbled.

"Alex found something, up in Saqqara, and he cabled us about it."

"Damn! We passed Saqqara on the way down here! Why didn't you tell us this while we were in Cairo, man?"

"Easy, Edward," Charlie soothed. "Lady Sarah will lose the time, too. We can just catch the train back."

"We didn't know you were coming, now did we, Eddie? You should have cabled me. My lips are sealed as well. Miss Brown may poke around all she likes, but I will tell her nothing. Davies and I are the only ones who know of his find. It's a tomb, up in the Saqqara necropolis. He says it's undisturbed and worth a fortune to the museum. The only other thing he would say was 'manicurists.' Does that mean anything to you?"

Edward shook his head. "Not a blessed thing. If he's there, we'll find him."

"I know you will. You've bought yourself some extra time. Now, there is no need for haste, so do not push yourself." He whacked his hat against the sand. "You take care of this stubborn knucklehead, Mr. Doyle. I'll call on you two when I get back to London next winter."

"Walker, take one of the camels. And a saddle. It'll save you time and I think you can use the beast."

Charlie heard him collect Davies and a camel, then start the ten-mile trek back to the Valley.

Edward squeezed Charlie a little tighter. "Thank you."

"You rest. I'll get some food around and when you feel better, we'll move back north and catch the train." He looked down, worriedly. "Can I catch this stuff?" Better to ask late than never.

"No, I'm not contagious. It comes from mosquitoes." He held up a finger. "But use your netting. A mosquito that bites me can transmit it to you."

"Yes, sir." Charlie bent and kissed him. "I'll make you something nice."

"Good luck on that score," Edward muttered as Charlie stoked up the charcoal burner and started opening cans.

# CHAPTER 5

# SAQQARA

**Some** say lovemaking is like flying. I have done both and they are nothing alike. Lovemaking is the most grounded experience I know; just two bodies, together, open to each other and a little afraid of what comes next.

—From the journal of Charles Doyle, secretary to Lord Withycombe

*****

Three days later, the morning sun found them again in Cairo.

Charlie packed their things and woke Edward for bread and jam. He was pleased to see his employer doing so much better. He'd insisted on riding to catch the train the day after Dr. Walker's visit, and Charlie had been hard pressed to keep him in the saddle. Edward had sweated and been feverish all the way to Cairo, sleeping much of the trip, but this morning he looked much better. Still tired, true, but his temperature had broken in the night.

They disembarked and headed back to the hotel room Edward rented in Cairo. Charlie was looking forward to using his typewriter for a while. He'd been writing up their adventure as a dime novel and hoped to serialize it in the papers. A hundred and fifty dollars a month felt like a fortune, especially with his housing and meals provided, but he knew money could evaporate quickly. Another income stream might be an excellent idea, especially if Edward was as wastrel as Robert had led him to believe.

Charlie clacked away, the ceiling fan stirring the hot desert air, while Edward paced in the next room, arguing with someone on the telephone. He finished three pages before Edward came back in and sat.

Charlie took stock. Edward was still too pale, but the fever showed no signs of returning. He'd be all right, but Charlie kept pushing water and food on him, trying to help him recover the strength he'd lost.

"Did you get more money?" Charlie asked. Edward had not been frugal with their advance and they were broke. The trip to the Valley of the Kings had cost dearly, both in time and money.

"A little. We'll just have to live on tinned rubbish and whatever we can scrounge at the bazaar until we get back to civilization." Edward looked glum. Charlie knew Edward hated canned food, having eaten so much during the War.

"I have a little bit of a story done up. If I can find an English newspaper, maybe they'd pay."

Edward barked a laugh. "Good luck with that. The only bright spot to the damned detour is that Sarah is now out of our hair. We'll ride over to Saqqara tomorrow and see what we can find."

Charlie covered his typewriter. He went and knelt beside Edward's chair and wrapped his arms around Edward's waist. "I have been having the most unprofessional and improper thoughts about you. Spending a day and a half in the desert being your hot water bottle has only intensified them."

Edward reached down and stroked his hair. "My thoughts, when not filled with delirium, have been most improper as well. What do you suggest we do about them?"

Charlie pulled him closer for a kiss, taking his time and enjoying it. His whole body tingled from the contact of their mouths. "A little of this, a little of that." He gave a half-sob as Edward thumbed his nipples through his shirt. "A whole lot of that. Whatever it is men do, when they love each other in the Greek way."

Edward rose and Charlie stood up. Edward wrapped his arm around Charlie's waist and stole a quick kiss. And then he pushed him away very gently. "Not here, Charles and not now. When we are safe in England or at least Europe."

Charlie swallowed, trying to get moisture back into a mouth that was suddenly very dry. He tried not to look downcast. He laid his fingers on Edward's chest, over the tattoo, over Edward's heart. "I understand."

Edward held him a moment. "In due time, my dear."

"My lord?" He was almost sure he didn't mean to sound quite so possessive on that phrase, but he tried again. "Edward, what comes next?"

"Tomorrow we go to Saqqara and find the missing Sir Alex. When Miss Brown arrives, hot, exhausted, and furious after barging halfway to Cush and back, we hustle Sir Alex aboard the ship for home and salute her properly." He brought two fingers up in a reverse V, a symbol of English defiance dating back to Agincourt when the longbowmen taunted the French that they still kept their shooting fingers.

Charlie laughed at that and kissed him again. "Nothing changes at all, then?"

"Only that you need no longer sleep on the sofa." Edward propped up on one elbow. "Charles, believe me when I say I never intended to seduce you. I hired you for your enthusiasm and brashness and kept you because you are splendid company."

Charlie kissed his neck. "I was hot for you the minute I left your New York office. I spent the half of the trip I wasn't seasick trying to figure out how to maneuver you into treating me as you did the maid. You always seem so amused when I write in my journal. I'm mostly writing about you."

Edward looked amused again. "I rather suspected as much. So you did overhear us in the closet? I'm a bit surprised you didn't join me."

Charlie tucked his head into Edward's shoulder and mumbled, "Kinda short of nerve and kinda long on seasickness that night."

Edward held him in, stroking him, until Charlie traced the lines of his tattoo. Charlie ran his fingers around the shape of the crown and then kissed the cockatrice. Edward drew a sharp breath.

"What do you write about me?" he asked, his attempt to move things to safer territory transparent.

"Everything. The way you light your pipe. The way the ends of your hair get all wavy when it's damp. Your habit of reading the social page of the *Times* first, as though you're making sure you haven't been caught in a scandal."

Edward's long fingers played in his hair. "This is a scandal. Absolutely illegal, not to mention the social stigma of taking up with the help. And not just the help, the American help of Irish extraction." He gave a soft laugh. "We'll be entirely proper in appearance. You'll have to unmake your bed every night before you come to mine."

Charlie looked up. "So I will be sleeping with you." He smiled at the thought. He'd expected to be told they could fool around, but that he would be sleeping alone for propriety's sake.

"You're not a whore, Charles, or a passing fancy to sate myself upon and then banish. I quite like you where you are. And I want you there every night." He kissed the top of Charlie's head. "Darling boy."

Charlie squirmed. "I'd, uh, rather you didn't call me that. All I hear is Lady Sarah sneering 'darling' at you every time you do."

"All right then. What shall I call you?"

Charlie thought a moment, his fingers idly circling Edward's nipple ring. "Anything Herself doesn't call you." He looked up and smiled. "I even like it when you call me Charles. And I never liked my full name."

"Charles it is, then." Edward tipped his face up and kissed him, looking a trifle disappointed.

"I'm sorry, sir," Charlie said. "I know you mean well and I like the endearment, but hearing 'darling' just sends shivers over me."

"It's settled, love," Edward said.

Charlie kissed his neck. "That I like."

Edward's hands moved in slow patterns on his back. "So do I. For I do love you."

Charlie knew this was not a man to whom such feelings, nor the admission of them, came easily. Edward was glib and flirtatious, but Charlie had never heard him express any affection to the ladies. As he lay there, in a hot Cairo hotel room, his bare skin sticking to Edward's, he realized exactly what he had been writing for all these weeks.

"I know you do, Edward. I love you, too, and have for weeks." Charlie rolled up and sealed it with a kiss.

"Good, that's settled." Edward's doting smile turned to a cheeky grin. "Now we can get on with the expedition. We'll have a nap and then find some dinner. We'll see whether we can acquire a map to Saqqara, but it's unlikely. Even if we find one, it will doubtless be inaccurate."

Charlie kissed his neck and cheek. "All right, that settles the expedition," he teased. "So what about women? Are they just fooling around or should I worry about competition?"

"I like women. I adore women. And more, I dream of sharing a woman with the man I love."

"Sharing, sir?"

"Indeed." Edward stroked Charlie, his low voice telling about all the ways two men could enjoy the same woman and each other.

Charlie dozed to the soft drone of Edward's voice and awakened to a room full of sunset and Edward's snoring. He still had some coins, so he ducked out to buy some bread to go with dinner. They might need to economize, but bread was only a few piastres.

He left a note and browsed the market stalls near their apartment. He had no fear. Lady Sarah and her cronies were four hundred miles away, learning nothing at all in the Valley of the Kings.

Charlie wandered the streets for the first time, being very careful not to get lost. He'd marked the route through the bazaar during the few trips with Edward on their way elsewhere, but he hadn't had time to just explore or to shop. He took it all in, the colors, the smells, the cries of the vendors.

He was definitely in Egypt. This was not New York or London, where great department stores displayed new merchandise behind enormous plate glass windows. Nor was it Harlow, with little shops lining the streets so one had to carry a basket from bakery to greengrocer. Here, strange fruit formed miniature pyramids under canopy awnings. Handmade jars and boxes and furniture, none of which had changed in design much from the museum pieces, gleamed and tempted. A jeweler kept an eagle eye on a tray of lapis necklaces and turquoise rings. The sellers' cries rang out, competing with each other in the cooling evening.

On one corner, an old man sat talking to a crowd of rapt children. The grown-ups ignored him and Charlie realized the old man spoke English. He listened, confused by this development, but intrigued by the story.

"So, Anubis and Khnum quarreled over the canopic jars, with each saying his were best. They brought it before a meeting of the gods, who decreed that the only way to determine the victor was to use each set of jars for a mummification. Now in those days, there lived two men, Khnum-ho-tep and Ni-ankh-khnum, both beloved of the potter god, manicurists to the pharaoh. Anubis, Lord of Death, took them. Ni-ankh-khnum was mummified using Anubis's jars. Khnum-ho-tep was mummified using Khnum's jars. Once both men had been interred, the gods called them up to answer the questions of who made the better canopic jars. They were quite unhappy to learn this was why their lives had been cut short and raged at Anubis. They denied that either set of jars was any good at all. This angered the gods. Khnum wept that his beloveds would so slander his work. Anubis, who claims all in his time, scowled and decreed they would not know the afterlife. So and the manicurists were trapped, prevented from moving on to the next world. They say even now, four thousand years later, Ni-ankh-khnum and Khnum-ho-tep—'He who lives in Khnum,' and 'Khnum is satisfied'—will neither live nor find satisfaction., They haunt their tomb, kin to the djinn and afreets and jackals, preying on the living, until they can be released."

The tale seemed to be winding down, so Charlie ventured on. Edward could tell a better ghost story. He bought a round loaf of fresh bread and some other things from the vendor, paying two English pennies and an American one. The vendor swore at him in Arabic and broken English, but Charlie gave him a grin. He knew what bread cost. He stored up the sound of the words to use next time he shopped. He tried some of the Arabic words Edward had taught him and the vendor grinned, too. They went back and forth for a minute, until Charlie dropped a piastre, worth about another cent, in the merchant's hand and thanked him for the new words.

He paused to watch a pretty girl with flashing dark eyes as she danced on a street corner. He dropped a single coin, less than the price of the bread, into the bowl at her feet and she sent him a smile. Only a couple of men were paying attention, so he stopped and watched a little more closely. She noticed and danced to him, her bare feet so light they barely seemed to touch the worn carpet she had spread as a makeshift stage. Her anklets jingled and the finger cymbals chimed in his ears, making him want to join her. A bowl sat on the corner of her rug and Charlie watched men toss silver coins in.

She spun away from him, to the opposite edge and kissed one of the watching men, a tall man wearing a bright blue vest with gold embroidery. Charlie watched her dainty henna-patterned hands come up on the sides of his face and press him to her after she unhooked one side of her veil. She lingered there, her feet and hips still moving, as the man moaned and shuddered. She released him and he sank to his knees as she danced away.

Edward's words about women echoed in Charlie's head. How would it be, Charlie wondered, having a woman that he wanted, not just one that wanted him as a trophy. The idea of having the dancer, with Edward there to help him and guide him along, consumed him. He checked his wallet. Edward might be broke, but he still had a bit of his salary. He'd left most of his money in London, not expecting to need it, since this was a working trip. There hadn't been much chance to spend it.

She whirled toward him and then away, a cloud of myrrh and cassia from her veils fuddling his head. He dug in his own purse and took out a whole dollar bill. It was probably more than he should spend, especially since they might need every nickel before the end of the trip, but he wanted something special for Edward. She saw and he beckoned her over. When she drew close, he held up the bill and tried to negotiate in sign language.

She got the idea he wanted her and nodded. He held up two fingers and pointed to himself and then gestured, indicating a taller man. She smiled and linked her arm into his.

He entered the apartment, bread in one hand, girl on the other arm. Her name was Safi and she called him "Shar-lee," making it almost two words. They hadn't managed anything else in the way of communication. She spoke no English and he spoke a dozen words of Arabic, four of them food, six numbers, and two really foul curses he'd picked up from the baker. Learning from a military man had its drawbacks, he decided, and planned to buy a phrasebook for whatever country they visited next.

Once back in the hotel room, he set the bread on the table and had Safi sit down while he went to find Edward. His employer was up and shaving. Charlie took the razor from his hand before he cut himself.

"Sit down," Charlie ordered. "You're still shaky." He rinsed the razor and stropped it. "How much Arabic do you speak?"

"Not much more than I taught you." Edward watched Charlie, but relaxed when Charlie started to shave him.

"I have a girl." Charlie pulled the straight razor over his skin with a brisk motion. "She came with me for a dollar. She's beautiful, a street dancer. Teach me?"

Edward looked at him as Charlie wiped the soap off his face. "A girl? Here?"

"Yes, she's in the sitting room. I went out for bread and came back with her, too." He hesitated. "Are you angry with me, sir?"

"Oh no, quite the contrary." Edward smiled and pulled Charlie down to pat his face. "What would you like to tell her?"

"That I think she is very beautiful and that my master and I would like to make love to her until the sun sets and rises again."

Edward looked puzzled for a moment. "I'm afraid that's quite beyond my scope. We'll just have to show her."

"I hope you like her, sir. I saw her dancing and thought of what you said this afternoon." Charlie led the way into the sitting room.

Safi sat where he'd left her. She smiled at him, her dark eyes enticing. "Shar-lee." She held her arms open and Charlie went to her, breathing her perfume of myrrh and spice. Edward held back a little.

Charlie had reached her and was about to kiss her when Edward bolted across the room and thrust a flaming lucifer into her swirling veils.

Charlie dropped her arm and recoiled as she went up in flame, far too fast, burning more like dry paper than like a human being. The flames consumed her veils. Her hair singed and shriveled away. Her lovely face went dry and gray, her mouth open in a scream that had no sound behind it. She turned accusatory empty eye sockets at Charlie as the dry grayness turned to ash. In bare minutes, only dried ash and a whisper of myrrh remained. The wooden seat of the chair wasn't even scorched. A small golden pendant in the shape of a pot lay on the chair.

Edward gestured to a mirror that was angled so he could see the door in it. "Always use a silver mirror in strange countries, Charles. You never know what might follow you home."

Charlie stood, his mouth hanging open and his eyes wide. He stammered out, "I brought her home, Edward. Dessert for us to share." The speed with which the girl had burnt, just up in flames, left him gaping. He sat down hard on the floor, the movement stirring the air and her ashes.

Charlie wasn't sure why Edward had incinerated the girl, nor how she had burnt so fast, like an ancient scroll. Even wood took a bit to catch and burned for a while. His uncle, the mortician, had once said that humans burned greasy and left bones behind. His mother had shushed Uncle Mike, but Charlie had never forgotten it..

He reached over picked up the still-cool necklace from the unmarked chair. "Was she even real?" He looked at Edward, wavering between fear, horror, confusion, and disappointment.

"She was real and quite beautiful. and I commend your taste. However, that, dear Charles, was a mummy. A lesser minion, to be sure, or she'd never have succumbed to a simple match. Don't gape at me, lad. We're in Egypt now, not England. Things are different here." He tamped down a nut of tobacco and lit his pipe. "There are still a great many strange things in odd corners of the world. Not every place is so tamed as England or New York."

Charlie rose to open a window and turned the fan's speed up to clear the room of the fragrant smoke. He sat down hard, still staring at the necklace, not really understanding. "At least I got bread for dinner, huh?" was all he could think of to say. Banal, true, but an attempt to return to whatever normal was in a world where dead girls danced in the street and burned in an instant.

"That you did." Edward looked underwhelmed at the prospect of dinner. He smoked his pipe thoughtfully.

The look reminded Charlie of his shopping trip, and he held up the other items he'd acquired: a string of onions, a melon, and some garlic and pepper. "Let's see if I can whip something up out of those cans." He chopped and stirred and fried and came up with a pretty decent corned beef hash. The activity of cooking let him not think about the fact he had brought a dead girl home. "A little hot sauce would make it perfect, but salt and pepper are fine," he said as he dished it out.

Edward took a hesitant, mechanical bite. After a taste, he brightened a bit and ate enthusiastically. "Congratulations, Charles," he said, smearing a piece of the bread with plum-apple jam, "you've done the impossible."

Charlie gave him a smile. "Does it make up for bringing a dead girl home?"

"Entirely, my dear."

"So how do I know which girls are real girls and which are dead?"

"Ask to meet her father." Edward helped himself to the end of the hash. "And be prepared to run when you do." His grin did not dissolve as he finished dinner and he even did the dishes so Charlie didn't have to.

Charlie made a journal entry and wrote about ten column inches for a paper while Edward washed up. Maybe tomorrow, he'd have a chance to check with the papers. He didn't want to talk about Safi. His head ached at the thought of a mummified corpse impersonating a street dancer. He didn't even want to know how it had been done. He was just very glad he hadn't kissed her.

He looked up to see Edward going out for a walk. "Wait for me, sir." Charlie grabbed his hat and caught the door.

"Just an evening constitutional, Charles. You didn't have to come along. I'm feeling almost myself again."

"Rather you were feeling me," Charlie suggested.

"Naughty," Edward scowled. "Discretion, Charles. We'll have a scandal yet and I shall have to move to America."

"You can live with me. I'll just have to get a double bed," Charlie said cheerfully. He paused to watch several dancers, then shook his head. "Just looking, sir."

Edward grinned in spite of himself. "Good. Keep looking. We'll enjoy the company of a pretty French girl soon enough." Charlie walked with him, learning the neighborhood. As they headed back, his arm started tingling and he scratched it idly.

"What's our next move?"

"Saqqara. I hope to be done fairly soon." Edward stared at where he was scratching. "Do you have a rash, Charles?"

Charlie looked down, where he had clawed himself red. He saw only his own nail marks. "I don't think so. I just itched. Probably the heat."

Edward took his arm, careful not to touch any of the area where he'd scratched, and brought it up to examine it more closely. "Is that where she touched you?"

Charlie thought. "Maybe? I don't remember. I was kinda busy thinking about where I was going to touch her. And how she was going to look with both of our hands on her."

They turned back toward the apartment and Charlie stopped dead. From the shadows of an alleyway, a desiccated arm dragged an equally shriveled body into the light. The dying man in the blue vest with gold embroidery crumpled at their feet, one palm raised imploringly as if begging for alms. He crumbled into gray ash and dry bones as they watched.

Edward turned to see Charlie staring. "I saw him watching her dance. She kissed him," Charlie whispered. His eyes wouldn't move from the pile of crumbling bones.

"Charles," Edward tugged lightly on the arm he still held.

"She only kissed him." Charlie almost reached down to touch the remains, seeming in a trance.

"No, Charles." Edward pulled him away and didn't let go of him as he dragged Charlie back to the hotel in double-quick time. "Into the bath with you. Immediately."

"Yes, Edward." Charlie stripped quickly and climbed into the bathtub. He wanted a bath after all that had happened today. Maybe it would help get his head clear.

Edward ran water that was far hotter than Charlie found comfortable and handed him a bar of strong, foul-smelling soap. "Scour. All over, but especially where you're itching."

Charlie obeyed, his nose wrinkling. The soap smelled worse than the lye stuff his grandma cooked up in the big iron kettle over an open fire. He washed twice and three times under Edward's watchful eye and realized he was naked for the first time in front of Edward, and being looked at. Deflection seemed better than allowing embarrassment or other, more prurient ideas, get the better of him. And the part of him that loved ghost stories and weird tales was wide awake and likely to keep him up all night with questions. "Is that how she stayed pretty? Eating the men who watched her and kissed her?"

"Your arm, Charles," Edward sighed. "Your surmise is probably correct but, for the moment, quell your curiosity, and make sure you get that arm."

Charlie washed the arm again and gasped. He held it up. "Look, don't touch."

The red place had turned gray and started to wrinkle. Little bits of skin flaked away when Charlie washed it. Edward scowled. "This isn't good."

"You're telling me. It doesn't hurt and it's quit itching. What is it, sir?" Charlie didn't want to imagine the dead man in the alley, but all he could see behind his eyes was that upturned reaching hand, the gray fingers crumbling like sand.

"I don't know." Edward dried his arm and wrapped a bandage around it, very careful not to touch the affected area. "You can be grateful it's not in a more sensitive area, though."

Charlie shot an unconscious glance downward. The image of those parts turning gray and shriveling made him shudder. He caught a tremor from Edward as well from the corner of his eye.

"Maybe I'd better sleep on the sofa until we're sure it's just that one patch," he suggested. He remembered what he'd read in the museum. "Mummy rot! I read about it when you were talking to the curator. I think it's mummy rot. But you were done before I could read how to cure it."

"That couch might be a wise idea." Edward frowned, looking distinctly unhappy about it. "I will miss you, love."

Charlie started to kiss him, but drew back. "We'd better wait and find out how contagious this is between humans. If it is. Can we call the museum and ask what the rest of the information says?" He got up and dried off, not using the towel Edward had used on his arm.

"Charles, you've lost track of the days. It's Friday. The museum will not reopen until Monday."

Charlie hung up the towel. "And I'll just bet it says something silly like it can only be cured by the mummy who inflicted it."

"We leave for Saqqara very early, then. I have a feeling our answers are there, probably in the form of Sir Alex." Edward kissed him, a light buss on the lips, before leaving him. "When you are well, and we are back to civilization, we will make up for all the lost time."

"I'm looking forward to that." Charlie put on Edward's nightshirt, although he had pajamas of his own now, and curled up on the sofa.

Throughout the night, Charlie heard Edward tossing and wanted to go in and check on him, to make sure he wasn't relapsing. After about an hour, he got up and almost bumped into Edward, who was coming to check on him.

"Charles." Edward touched his hair, brushing it out of his eyes. "I'm sorry. I didn't mean to disturb you."

"I was worried," Charlie said. "You kept thrashing around." He looked Edward over for telltale sweating. "Are you relapsing?"

"Not if you're not going all gray and dead."

Charlie checked his arm. There was no sign of the disease spreading beyond the bandage. "I'm still pink."

Edward nodded and turned back to his bedroom. Charlie blurted, "Should I sleep beside your bed so you can hear me breathe?"

"You're not a dog. You don't have to sleep on the floor."

Charlie grabbed his blanket and pillow. "I'll sleep better if I can hear you breathe, too."

"Get in the bed. If I catch it, I catch it, and we'll find the cure together," Edward decided. Charlie crawled in and Edward immediately wrapped around him and kissed his neck. "We may make a slightly later start. Pack when we get up, please, Charles."

"Yes, sir." Charlie yawned.

*****

Morning found them on horseback headed south to the necropolis of Saqqara. They had swapped the remaining camel for horses since Saqqara was near Cairo and on main roads. Edward studied the rough map and the copy of the cable that Dr. Walker had given him.

"Pots," he mumbled over and over. The rest of the cable made sense, but the lone word, "pots," stood in the middle, apropos of nothing. The desert shimmered in the morning haze and they covered the twenty miles easily.

Based on the map, Edward guided them to the easternmost edge. "It should be here somewhere," he said and then read the cable again. "New tomb. Changes everything. Pots. Manicurists.-The first part makes sense. The second part must be about the tomb itself."

They searched the edges of Saqqara, checking the ruins for anything that looked like a tomb involving pots or manicurists. Charlie could read a few hieroglyphics, which he'd picked up as a lark one summer when he'd been fascinated by codes. Edward could read a very few, just from having knocked around Egypt after the war.

"What is it with bloody pots?" Edward grumbled to himself. They kept looking.

When the sun rose high, beating down on them, they moved into the shade of a half-buried tomb to eat a bite of lunch and have a drink.

"We'll take up the search when the day cools." Edward leaned back against some fallen stones, making sure to catch the breeze. Charlie joined him, tracing his fingers over the half-obscured carvings.

They rested and Charlie puzzled out what was on the rock.

"I think I have it." The pot, the ankh, and the eye with a comb all seemed to fall into place.

"What do you have?" Edward asked sleepily.

"Our pots and maybe the manicurists, too. Damn, I wish I knew more hieroglyphics." Charlie tapped the stone, and blew away some sand. The wind had kicked up a little and blew more into its place. "See? A pot and what looks like a cosmetic thing. We're right where we should be."

"But where would that be?" Edward looked around for more clues. "There's a bit of a doorway. We'll have to crawl to get in. Not the wisest choice. We might end up trapped."

Charlie stood up and stared over at the far western horizon. A roiling dark cloud was growing larger by the moment. It looked like a raincloud, except that it went from ground to sky, filling the whole horizon. Charlie put his hand on his head to keep his pith helmet from blowing away in the wind. "We might be anyway. Is that a sandstorm, sir?"

Edward looked in the direction Charlie was pointing and swore. "No choice then. Charles, get everything we can carry." He scooped at the sand and debris in the tomb entrance, enlarging it for them.

Charlie grabbed all the water and the bags with the food. He got his own pack on and managed to lug Edward's to safety. He ducked inside the tomb just as the first spicules of sand scored his cheeks. Edward had found a fair-sized chamber and was using the end of the daylight and their electric torch to explore it.

Charlie looked at the painting on the wall. Two men sat together on a bench with their arms around each other. The hieroglyphics on the wall showed a pot by each one's face. The one on the left had an ankh and a wavy line and the one on the right had a little dome and a rectangle. Below them, smaller servants brought various offerings, including a peacock, a platter mounded with bread, and an overflowing jar of oil.

Edward stepped on something that snapped and he aimed the torch down. Charlie gasped, dropping Edward's pack and causing more crunches.

"Oh, bloody hell," Edward swore. He brushed aside sand and Charlie saw it was the remains of a body. They swept away enough sand to expose the bush cottons and a desiccated corpse. It had been here long enough that it no longer smelled strongly of decay.

Charlie came to Edward's side and picked up a book lying by the corpse's side. "A diary, Edward." He read, "Trapped by a sandstorm, I found the tomb of Ni-ankh-khnum and Khnum-ho-tep, Overseers of the Manicurists in the Palace of the Pharaoh. The Pharaoh is doubtless Niuserre of the Fifth Dynasty. Food and water low and my shelter is not as stable as it could be if the grinding of the stones is any indication. The place feels occupied, in a way most tombs do not, as if these men left their essence on this plane." He flipped to the front. "It's Sir Alexander Spencer."

Edward had examined the body. "Not stable, indeed." He indicated a large chunk of rock from the ceiling that had fallen and smashed Sir Alex's skull. "Poor bastard."

Charlie helped him He wrapped Sir Alex's body in a blanket from the packs and they settled it with their gear. *Mission accomplished*, Charlie thought with a small surge of triumph. Now all that remained was getting him back to England.

"We'll get you back home, old man." Edward spared a worried glance at the ceiling to check the current stability.

By the light of the electric torch, Charlie examined the painting on the south wall. The painted men held hands as they led the visitors deeper into the tomb, overseeing the building of it. Their faces had flaked away over the years, but the touching hands remained, sweet as the day they'd been painted.

"Don't wander, love. I don't want to lose you, too." Edward joined him, but Charlie barely heard him. The hieroglyphics seemed almost readable, just about to coalesce into something he understood.

Charlie felt distinctly odd as he stared at the paintings, trying to decipher them. The painted figures swam in and out of focus and his head whirled. From the corner of his eye, he saw Edward sit down hard, on the sandy ground for no apparent reason, the torch dropping from his fingers.

The tomb went black.

*****

The reed torches on the wall flared to life. Khnum-ho-tep sat up and looked around with living eyes. There were odd memories of being someone called Charlie or Charles. Beside him, Ni-ankh-khnum—looking much different—shook his head and crawled over to him.

"Are you well, my love?"

"Better than the day they laid me beside you." Khnum-ho-tep embraced his lover and touched noses in a kiss, just as he had made the tomb artists paint them in the inner chamber.

"I have missed touching you." Ni-ankh-khnum held him for a long moment, and touched his nose again. "You look so different, love."

Khnum-ho-tep traced the small mustache above his beloved's mouth. "As do you. You never had this before." He stroked the thick, wavy hair. "Yours was always shaved and it was black and curled tightly." He paused and touched the odd bits of clear stone that sat before his eyes. When he took them off, the world and even his beloved Ni-ankh-khnum went blurry, as if seen through water or a heat shimmer. "And these." He put them back on and could see clearly again.

"The bodies are only borrowed," Ni-ankh-khnum reminded him. "I don't know why or for how long."

"How do we end this interminable exile? I will have forgotten all of my family's Book, and not be able to find my path in the afterlife."

"We must appease the gods, somehow. Khnum and Anubis and perhaps Osiris so he may compel Anubis to let us pass, if he is not inclined." Ni-ankh-khnum stroked his lover's new body, shoving away the top layer of clothing, so badly woven from poor cotton, and scowled at a second layer of cloth. "I wish to hold you properly and all I find is another barrier. This clothing is ridiculous."

Khnum-ho-tep drew a little away. "Time is not our friend. These men will want their bodies back. How do we appease the gods?"

"We need Khnum to hear us again. He turned his face from us at our rash words after death." Ni-ankh-khnum paced through the tomb chamber.

Khnum-hot-tep remembered he had always been better at the religious rituals than his lover. "We were angry. Time may have soothed his pain, as it has soothed our wrath. Khnum, lord of the water, the uniter. What better offering could we make to him than water and a union of ourselves?"

Ni-ankh-khnum chuckled. "He is dead for four thousand years and suddenly he is the husband."

Khnum-ho-tep gestured to the painting of him offering Ni-ankh-khnum a lotus., Many wives were painted the same way in the tombs they shared with their husbands. "Water, prayers, and then sacred loving, that Khnum may hear us and lift the curse."

"Can he do so when Anubis laid it upon us?"

"He can at least gain us hearing with Anubis. Perhaps, after four thousand years, even the Lord of the Embalming Chamber can forgive."

"We can hope." Ni-ankh-khnum held up a waterskin. "Some things have not changed." He took a drink. "Sweet, if a bit warm."

Khnum-ho-tep found a pot and a bowl. He knelt before a painting of the potter god, the ram's-headed man, seated at his wheel, making pots and small children of the clay, with stacks of both beside him. Ni-ankh-khnum brought him the waterskin and filled the pot.

Khnum-ho-tep poured water from the pot into the bowl and chanted the Morning Hymn to Khnum, which seemed quite appropriate. It might not be morning, but he and Ni-ankh-khnum were just awakening. Given the millennia they had slept, it was possible that Khnum needed to be awakened too.

> "Wake well in peace, wake well in peace,
> Khnum-Amun, the ancient,
> Issued from Nun,
> In peace, awake peaceably!
>
> "Wake, Lord of Fields,
> Great Khnum,
> Who makes his domain in the meadow,
> In peace, awake peaceably!
>
> "Wake, Lord of Gods and Men,
> Lord of the war cry,
> In peace, awake peaceably!
>
> "Wake, mighty planner,
> Great Power In Kemet,

In peace, awake peaceably!"

Khnum-ho-tep trailed off. He looked at his lover, dismay and shock spreading over his face. "I've forgotten the next verse."

Ni-ankh-khnum smiled. "It's all right. I think he'll understand. Do you remember the end of it?"

Khnum-ho-tep took the seeing stones from his eyes and shook his head. He hated the way everything blurred, like a smudged painting, but he couldn't stand clarity right now either. He flushed red, embarrassed that he, who had led his own household and the manicurists in the palace of the Pharaoh in morning prayers, could not now remember the most basic.

"Time robbed me of it." He put the eyes back on. "How will we find the afterlife or speak to the gods if I cannot remember?"

"I remember the end." Ni-ankh-khnum knelt beside him and took his hand. "We will be fine, love." He poured a few drops of water in the bowl.

"Wake, Fighting Ram Who Chases His Foes,
Herdsman of his Followers,
In peace, awake peaceably!
"Wake, Multiform One,
Who Changes Shape at Will,
In peace, awake peaceably!
"Wake, Khnum Who Fashions as He Wishes,
Who sets every man in his place!"

"Do you really think he'll hear us, after all this time and his great sadness?" Khnum-ho-tep looked at the bowl of water, just a bit of clay sitting on sand in front of a painted wall. He ached with the thought of losing the afterlife. Fear that there had never really been one to start with had begun to grow within him, the seeds of doubt blooming quickly into thick vines, choking his mind.

Ni-ankh-khnum said nothing, but held his hand a little tighter. His lover had never been a deeply religious man. Ni-ankh-khnum was a sensualist and a creature of his senses. He hadn't actually expected an afterlife, Khnum-ho-tep realized.

"Do you think the Great Hymn would help?" Ni-ankh-khnum asked after a while spent in silence.

Khnum-ho-tep smiled in spite of himself. He said what he had always said when they lived. "You only know that one because it talks about phalluses, four times."

Ni-ankh-khnum returned the smile. "We have made the offering of water and song. Now, the offering of unity. For Khnum shaped all of our bodies, and directs us all in our love."

Khnum-ho-tep leaned in and touched noses. It couldn't hurt to try. If nothing else, being incorporeal for four thousand years had left him missing touch more than he expected.

Ni-ankh-khnum pushed aside all the layers of clothing these strange new bodies wore. Khnum-ho-tep helped, confused by the cut and the fasteners, so different than their own elegantly draped cotton and linen. Soon enough, Ni-ankh-khnum's hands were touching all the old remembered places and Khnum-ho-tep found this body liked it as well as his own had.

They found a blanket among the packs and spread it over the stone bed in the offering chamber. Ni-ankh-khnum touched noses and then brushed his fingers over Khnum-ho-tep's body.

"Delayed only slightly by death, my dearest," he said. He went to a place in the wall and touched the hidden drawer. Finding an alabaster jar, he picked it up and opened it. The fragrant oil, full of lotus, filled the chamber with scent. He poured some into his palm and stroked it over Khnum-ho-tep. Apparently someone approved of their union. Oil should not have kept so long.

Khnum-ho-tep smiled at his lover and ran slow fingers over the strange and pale body. "Did I choose well?"

"Indeed, and Safi did her work as well." Ni-ankh-khnum smiled and slid one oiled finger into Khnum-ho-tep's body.

Khnum-ho-tep frowned. "It hurts. It never hurt before."

"The boy is a likely virgin, dearest. Do you not remember your first?" Ni-ankh-khnum withdrew and rubbed more oil over the opening.

His first lover had been long before, but Khnum-ho-tep remembered. "Even that did not hurt." He smiled when Ni-ankh-khnum tried again. "Better."

Gently, his lover prepared the resisting body, a process Khnum-ho-tep found tedious. They had been men and lovers for twenty years together before Anubis took them, yet here his borrowed body behaved like a virgin youth's or a timid bride refusing to admit the rightful husband. He wondered if this would do anything more than leave him sore.

Ni-ankh-khnum kissed him and kept on until Khnum-ho-tep took three fingers without pain. Khnum-ho-tep looked at his lover's penis, much larger on this body than he had been in life. "Will it fit?"

"If I am gentle." Ni-ankh-khnum lay beside him and curled around him. Khnum-ho-tep rested in his lover's arms, having missed this touch most of all.

Very carefully, Ni-ankh-khnum pressed at his opening, adding more oil and pressing, waiting for Khnum-ho-tep to open for him. Khnum-ho-tep gave a small sigh as his lover entered and rocked back, swallowing him up with his body.

"Just as I remembered it," Ni-ankh-khnum whispered. "My beloved."

"Always gentle, my lover." Khnum-ho-tep pressed his nose to his lover's, lingering.

They lay together, savoring the remembered pleasures, indulging in the new ones. With the knowledge only those who have loved one another for years have acquired, they explored, only to find the new bodies responded differently than they recalled.

"Delightful." Ni-ankh-khnum sighed. "All is new and yet, you, my beloved, have not changed within."

Light gleamed around the edges of what the masons had believed was a false door, glowing brighter than the torches around them. Many tombs were built with such doors, the real work done by priests after builders had left. It was not a false door, but one that existed only partially in the Land of the Living. Khnum-ho-tep stared, the light becoming hope that withered the vines of doubt as the sun shriveling a gourd vine.

The light grew brighter and the door opened. A man with long curling horns stood silhouetted in the brightness.

Ni-ankh-khnum rose up, leaving the borrowed body behind on the stone bed. Khnum-ho-tep followed him. As they approached the door, the god Khnum nodded. They could see his face and his smile.

Khnum-ho-tep kissed him. "The offering of Unity is accepted. And so we complete what we began on the day Khnum and Anubis quarreled. Now, perhaps, we can go to what awaits us, instead of hovering over an empty tomb."

*****

Charlie shook his head at the voices he was hearing. The next voice was Edward's, but the words were all wrong. "My love?" he asked, tipping back to look, only realizing then that they lay on a stone slab and—

He gasped. Edward moved more slowly within him. "Khnum-ho-tep, beloved, is it hurting again?" The inflections were all wrong.

"Uh, no, not at all." He lay perfectly still trying to sort out everything he felt. Stone beneath him, Edward inside him, and his glasses still on. He tried to believe he'd imagined the strange words. His whole body tingled, his nerves crawling with heatless fire. When Edward moved gently and soothed him with sweet words in a language he somehow knew to be Ancient Egyptian and still half-understood, he relaxed. He tipped his face back and bumped noses with his lover.

They had planned to do this, once they were back, but it seemed things had gone awry., Charlie could find no good way to extricate himself from the situation and he wasn't in pain and didn't object. So he lay in Edward's arms, and let the lovemaking continue.

"Damnably awkward, now, isn't this?" Nigel sneered from the doorway, pistol leveled at them. "You disoriented, him possessed, and both absolutely starkers." He smirked a little. "So it's true what they say about American weaponry after all."

Charlie yanked the side of the blanket up to cover himself and glanced back at Edward, who blinked as if in a daze. Finding no help from that quarter, he returned Nigel's smirk. "Be that as it may, I'm the one who's where you want to be."

"Charles? What?" Edward kissed Charlie's neck and then stopped, raising his head slowly. "Nigel." The word held no affection.

"So sorry to interrupt, love. But there was this ghastly sandstorm and when we took shelter, well, well, look what we found."

Lady Sarah stepped into the chamber, following the sound of Nigel's voice. "Oh, how lovely. Don't let us interrupt, Edward, darling. We checked your belongings when we arrived. When the storm blows over, we'll just take Sir Alex's body and you can continue taking your secretary's body."

"We were first, Miss Brown, fair and square," Edward growled. They hadn't yet parted or reached for their clothes, although Charlie had lost all interest in sex.

"Yes, you were. But we're better armed. Please," she gestured at Charlie, "continue. You know how I love watching."

"Didn't seem to enjoy it so well when it was the cook's assistant. I remember a frying pan coming at me for that," Edward taunted, moving backward, leaving Charlie's body.

Charlie squirmed away and cast about for their clothes. He seemed to remember leaving them in the banquet chamber. He encouraged Edward to sit up, only to find his lover attempting to stare down Nigel.

He gasped when Nigel broke the stare, took three quick steps over, and seized him by the throat, putting the gun to his head. He fought as Nigel dragged him out of Edward's reach.

"My lord!" he squeaked.

Edward's eyes never left Nigel's gun. Very slowly, he sat up and covered himself with the blanket, keeping his hands in sight.

"Ah, Edward, so very formal of him," Nigel taunted. "You must be losing your touch." He settled his back to the wall, Charlie in front of him, with his arm around Charlie's throat and the cold muzzle next to Charlie's temple. "I suggest you do exactly as my lady says."

"Sir Alex is yours. Now unhand my secretary!"

Charlie thrilled at the possessive anger in Edward's voice, even as he ached for the loss of their prize. He twisted away as Nigel whispered obscenities in his ear. Nigel jabbed him with the gun.

"Hold still or I'll shoot something you will miss, nonfatally," Nigel said. He added in a whisper, just for Charlie, "Edward has a liking for eunuchs. I've seen him enjoy them by twos. He wouldn't care if you were." He licked Charlie's neck again, showing off.

"Ah! Nigel has taken a liking to your boy," Lady Sarah beamed. "I'm sure he'd hate to have to blow that adorable head off. I rather like him myself. Perhaps I should take him along as a guarantee of your good behavior."

"You heard me," Edward warned, sweat standing out on his face. "Hand him over." Charlie saw a manic gleam in his eye. Apparently, Nigel did, too, because he cocked the gun.

"Be good, darling Edward," Lady Sarah's voice trailed back from the banquet chamber. "The storm's abating. You'll get the boy back, once I get paid."

Edward's eyes still gleamed and he was dangerously quiet as he slipped off the table and stalked toward Nigel. Nigel edged out the door, still holding Charlie.

"Back off, lover, or I put a bullet in him," Nigel warned.

"You shoot him and you will deal with me. I can break you in two."

Nigel gave a half-grin and caressed Charlie's face with the gun. "True, but I can shoot you just as easily." He pulled Charlie out into the banquet chamber. Khnum-ho-tep and Ni-ankh-khnum presided over the eternal feast painted on the wall.

"Hand him over," Edward repeated. He stopped at his clothing, dropped to one knee as if to get dressed, and seized his gun, abandoned with his clothes. He knelt, aiming it. took a brief second to aim, drawing a bead on Nigel's head.

"He's lovely." Nigel nuzzled Charlie's hair and Charlie pulled away from his touch. Nigel had moved the gun to the small of his back and jabbed him hard, a reminder to be obedient. "I'd like to have him one day." Nigel shoved Charlie straight into Edward's gun even as Charlie struggled to right himself. "But not today."

Charlie heard two pistol shots and Edward shouting. A burning pain filled his chest from front and back.

He felt very wet, even here in the desert, and realized it was blood. Edward stared down at him, stricken. Charlie reached up and bumped noses with him.

"I love you." The words took all he had and he tucked his head against Edward's shoulder to rest.

# CHAPTER 6

# ON THE OTHER SIDE

**The** Afterlife has been the source of much speculation since man first understood death. All I can say is there was too much beer and I remained my usual confused self through it all.

—From the journal of Charles Doyle, Secretary to Lord Withycombe

*****

Charlie sat up with a gasp and shook his head to clear it of the fog that had settled over him. The middle of his chest ached. Edward was nowhere to be seen. He'd been shot. Nigel had shoved him into Edward's gun, which had fired, and then shot him in the back. He wanted to scream and raged and cry and laugh to find he was still alive.

"Edward?" he said softly. If his employer was still nearby, he would answer, Charlie was sure.

No sound came to him, not even the rustle of sand or the wind outside. Edward had left him. Charlie lay back down. Edward knew he was dead and had left him here, not even troubling to take his body back to Cairo, let along England or America. That hurt. If he was dead, he might as well get on with being dead. He folded his arms across his chest as he remembered seeing his great-uncle laid out.

Apparently, being dead was really boring. Charlie couldn't remember the last time he had tried lying still and not thinking. He realized he could see his arms, just barely.

A faint light from the hallway kept the dark banquet chamber of the tomb from being pitch black. Since being dead wasn't accomplishing much, Charlie got to his feet carefully, realizing he was still naked, but somehow finding that unimportant. Walking took some effort, his feet feeling oddly numb. He held on to the wall and headed down the hall toward the light coming from inner chamber where it seeped from what they had determined was a false door.

He made his way to it and pressed his hand to the wall. The door swung open and he gawked.

Ni-ankh-khnum and Khnum-ho-tep sat at a table laden with fruits and bread and meat. Flutists and drummers played to one side and a pretty boy danced before them. They looked up when Charlie opened the door.

"Greetings and welcome to our house of eternity." Khnum-ho-tep stood up and beckoned him into the bright and joyous room.

Charlie came in and looked at them. He stared around himself at the celebration. "I'm dead," he said, by way of explanation. It sounded ridiculous, since dead people didn't walk and talk and get bored. Nor did they stumble into secret rooms in forgotten tombs. He probably wasn't dead, but just dreaming. He knew the Egyptians conceived of their afterlife as being like mortal life, only better, but he'd never expected to find himself in the middle of one or even in the middle of dreaming about one.

Ni-ankh-khnum nodded. "Yes. Rejoice with us."

Charlie blinked. He spoke less than a hundred words of Arabic and none at all of Ancient Egyptian. English hadn't even existed when the men before him had died. "How do we understand each other? You can't be speaking English."

Ni-ankh-khnum laughed, different than Edward's great rolling laugh, but similar nonetheless. "You speak excellent, if slightly accented, Egyptian."

It made no sense. But then again, he was dead and talking to men who had been dead for thousands of years. Quibbling about language was one of the more ridiculous things about the situation.

He clapped and a servant brought Charlie a cup of beer and another offered him bread and fruit.

Charlie, solidly in mind of the myth of Persephone, did not eat or drink. He held the cup and looked at his hosts. "But I'm not Egyptian. I'm not even of your beliefs."

"That doesn't matter. Khnum-ho-tep was still half within you." Ni-ankh-khnum gave him a wicked wink that was pure Edward. "And so was I."

Khnum-ho-tep frowned at his lover and took up the story. "Since I was still partially in possession, you came along when we were freed from the mortal plane. We only just got here."

They beckoned him to sit at the table with them. Charlie took a seat on a throne-like chair and watched the dancers, the boy giving way to a pair of girls who used each other as platforms for acrobatic tumbling before moving into more traditional forms. He set the beer down and watched, listening to the pipes and drums and even the clappers who reminded him of the men who played spoons and knucklebones back home. If this was being dead, he didn't mind too much for now.

He was definitely dreaming. They had fallen asleep in the tomb while the sandstorm raged and he was having a most bizarre dream.

"What if I don't want to be dead?" he asked. "Edward's waiting for me. I need to get back to him." As he said this, he knew it was true. He was quite sure now that Edward hadn't abandoned him. His employer was simply not appearing in this dream. He wanted to be with Edward, and not just because his employer had a way of making everything seem simple. He wanted to talk about how they had awakened and possibly ask for a reprise while they were both awake and in their own minds. He wanted to lay plans for revenge. He wanted Edward to teach him to shoot so he could settle with Nigel personally.

Now, all that seemed unlikely. And he wasn't sure how well he liked the Egyptian music, certainly not well enough to listen to it forever or even to the end of the dream.

A sudden darkness fell over the banquet and the roof opened up. A great, half-mummified man of sickly green complexion, carrying a crook and flail and wearing a white crown, appeared in the gap. All the servants fell on their faces and Charlie's hosts bowed low.

"Lord Osiris," Khnum-ho-tep gasped, awe and fear in his voice, as he pulled a gawking Charlie to bow before the great god as well.

"Bring the stranger to me," Osiris ordered. "He has not been weighed or found worthy."

Charlie watched, blinking as the ceiling replaced itself. He really was dead, or dreaming a lot. First dead manicurists, now actual old gods. Either way, nothing could hurt him. He stood up and Ni-ankh-khnum took his left side and Khnum-ho-tep took his right.

"Come with us, please, my friend," Khnum-ho-tep said.

Charlie did not resist as they led him out of the tomb into a transformed Saqqara. He thought hard about everything he'd ever heard or read about Ancient Egypt. He paid scant notice to the great white tombs rising from the sands around him, where there had been only ruins before. He could feel the looming insanity if he thought about his situation too hard and really believed it. He was dead and in an afterlife he didn't even believe in, going to be judged by a god he'd only read about. There was nothing in his Presbyterian Sunday School upbringing to account for this.

He really hoped it was a dream. Thinking of Edward still trapped in the tomb with his corpse made him ache clear through. He was dreaming. That was the best way to get through this. He'd just keep believing this was a long and detailed dream and that way he wouldn't start screaming. He would wake up, and Edward would have stolen both blankets and they would have sand in all sorts of uncomfortable places from sleeping in the desert. He'd have to check his pack for scorpions and they'd go back into Cairo for breakfast and head to England with poor Sir Alex.

When the manicurists led him into a large building that appeared to be a communal bath, he looked around in even more puzzlement. It didn't look like a temple. Was Osiris in the bathtub? If he was, would he take kindly to Charlie dragging him out of it?

"Is this the place to meet Osiris?" he asked.

"No, no, my friend," Khnum-ho-tep said. "You died without any rites or funeral, so we must prepare you to meet a god. A bath, a shave, some scent, and some clothes. Nakedness is solely for slaves."

Charlie looked down and remembered that he was still naked. "Yeah, all right. Since it's your fault I'm naked anyway."

Khnum-ho-tep had the grace to look embarrassed, but Ni-ankh-khnum just grinned. Apparently, some traits lingered, even after they had given the bodies back.

"Come now, handsome." Ni-ankh-khnum touched him lightly, just as Edward always did. "Into the bath. You're very dusty and still bloody. That won't do."

Charlie looked at his chest as he stepped onto the stone slab as they directed him. He saw blood all over his stomach, the bullet wound from Edward's gun, even some powder marks. Rough dream. He relaxed a little as Khnum-ho-tep poured the first bowl of water over him. Ni-ankh-khnum rubbed him with a sea sponge and some soft, sweet-smelling soap, getting the blood and sand and dirt off of his body.

Charlie looked down and saw the bullet holes had closed, leaving only a circular scar on his front. He twisted and groped until his fingers found its mate on his back.

"Do stop squirming. We shouldn't wish to drown you."

Khnum-ho-tep poured another basin over him. Charlie watched it drain out through holes in the slab.

"We're very grateful to you for allowing us to move on. Being stuck as unpleasant spirits haunting the tombs like hyenas didn't suit us. And we'd been out so long," Khnum-ho-tep said. "We do apologize for borrowing without permission, but Khnum knows when another opportunity would have presented itself. You are so clearly in love with your man that we knew you were the right ones."

Ni-ankh-khnum stroked Charlie's arm where Safi had infested him with the mummy rot. "Sweet little Safi. She marked you well for us. Shame your love incinerated her. I will miss watching her dance."

Khnum-ho-tep cleared his throat in warning. Charlie understood then that Ni-ankh-khnum had not merely watched the girl. He suspected Ni-ankh-khnum was a great deal like Edward, not all of it a holdover from possession, and that Khnum-ho-tep was the jealous kind.

Ni-ankh-khnum rubbed his arm a bit more and touched a scarab ring to it. "Let me get that off of you now. Did you like my sandstorm?"

"I would have liked it better if it hadn't dumped Lady Sarah in on us."

"Formidable woman," Khnum-ho-tep shuddered. "Reminds me of your last wife," he added to Ni-ankh-khnum, who pretended to ignore him. "I had her likeness chiseled off the wall for a reason."

"Jealous, jealous." Ni-ankh-khnum washed Charlie's hair with the same soap, marveling at its texture. "Softer than that of the Greeks, even. Where do you come from, dear friend?"

"My name's Charlie. I'm from America. It's over the ocean to the west."

The manicurists nodded to each other and dried him with soft linen. At their urging, Charlie sat down. Khnum-ho-tep rubbed him with ointment and dabbed scented oils on his palms, his knees and his groin. The attention awakened his body and he blushed at the response. The other men just smiled, clearly used to this happening during their work.

Ni-ankh-khnum stropped a bronze razor as Khnum-ho-tep rubbed oil along Charlie's jaw. Ni-ankh-khnum's deft touch flicked the razor over Charlie's face, giving him his closest shave ever. When Khnum-ho-tep oiled his armpits and Ni-ankh-khnum's razor flashed there as well, Charlie was too relaxed to worry. They took the hair from his chest and legs, but when Khnumho-tep started rubbing oil into his groin, Charlie protested.

"Hey! That, too?"

"Everything, little brother," Khnum-ho-tep said. "We will leave you your head hair. You have no need of a wig."

Charlie held his breath the whole time the half-moon shaped razor was on him. They were experts he reminded himself, and this was just a dream. Ni-ankh-khnum smiled up at him, tested the slickness of the shaved skin, and stood.

"Clothes and a perfume cone and he'll be ready," Ni-ankh-khnum said. When Khnum-ho-tep stepped out to get them, he leaned a little closer. "I remember being within you, Charlie. You were wonderful."

"Glad you think so, because I don't remember any of it, until I woke and Khnum-ho-tep went away."

"Your body is very beautiful, as is that of your lover. I was jealous of him. Now I feel pain for him, losing you. And for you, waiting here for him. It can be a long wait for your beloved." Ni-ankh-khnum patted his face and stepped away as Khnum-ho-tep returned.

Together they helped Charlie into a linen wrap like the ones they wore and Khnum-ho-tep pinned a wax cone atop his head. It smelled of cassia and frankincense, chrysanthemum, myrrh, and cedar. It melted a little from his body heat, making a sticky mess of his hair.

He let Khnum-ho-tep look over his nails, paring and buffing, while Ni-ankh-khnum lined his eyes with kohl. He felt bizarrely different and could almost believe he was really dead and not just dreaming.

"He is ready," Ni-ankh-khnum announced. Khnum-ho-tep looked Charlie over and agreed, before bumping noses with his lover.

"Perfect as always."

Khnum-ho-tep held up a bronze mirror. Charlie saw himself, no longer the journalism graduate who had needed to take a couple deep breaths before a job interview, nor even the eager explorer on his first trip out of the country. This Charlie looked like someone's lover, a pretty toy to be cuddled and played with. He wasn't sure he liked the changes. Part of him wished Edward was here, and the rest wanted to wake up.

Khnum-ho-tepHe tucked one arm into Charlie's and Ni-ankh-khnum took the other side. "In life, we had a dozen staff under us to do the work. Sometimes, it is pleasant to simply keep one's hand in."

After all of this, Charlie didn't quail as the pair set their feet on empty air and began climbing an invisible staircase. He held tightly to them, climbed, and did not look down. It was just a dream; he couldn't fall.

Up into the sky, black and glittering with low, fat stars, they climbed, moving toward one that grew ever brighter. Charlie saw shapes moving within and it became clear the star was a door, looking into a lit banquet hall.

Osiris sat at the place of honor, his mummified feet under the table, his flail and crook set to the side as he toasted his lovely wife, Isis. The goddess sat beside him, light glimmering over her golden vulture headdress, smiling on him.

The manicurists took Charlie in and all three went to their knees, Charlie a little uneasily. He worried about what would happen when Osiris found out he was a Christian, even if his faith had been pretty nominal. If he got sent over to God and he'd bowed to a heathen god… And there was being in love with Edward to consider too. It all made his head spin and he gave up thinking about it. He'd take his chances with Osiris.

"This is the new arrival," Osiris said. "Bring forth the Balance!"

The cry was taken up and a great golden scale appeared in the center of the hall, borne by a god with the head of a jackal. Charlie knew him to be Anubis, gatekeeper of death. Osiris stood beside Charlie, without having seemed to move.

"But, please, my lord Osiris, I'm not even one of your believers."

The green face smiled down at him. "It doesn't matter, child. Our children believed in you and you died while still halfway between the realms." He gestured to the manicurists. Anubis seemed to glower in that direction.

Charlie recoiled as a hideous monster, with the head of a crocodile, the body of a great cat, and the hindquarters of a hippopotamus came to sit beside the scale. The thing was terrifying enough that Charlie turned as if to bolt from the hall. Osiris stopped him with a gentle hand on his chest.

When the god withdrew his hand, Charlie's heart lay in it. Osiris addressed the heart.

"Do you swear, Charles Brian Doyle, not to have caused hunger or sorrow? Do you swear you have not killed nor made others kill for you? That you are no thief and have not stolen the food of the dead, nor the milk of babes, nor the cattle of the fields or the birds of the gods? Do you swear you have been honest and upright, using only fair weights and measures in all dealing?"

Charlie's heart, which lay unbeating in the god's hand, answered, "I do so swear, my lord Osiris." Charlie just stared mutely, waiting to see what else would happen. His heart didn't have a mouth, but the words had been clear.

Osiris laid Charlie's heart on one pan of the Balance. A single white feather rested on the other. The room held its breath as the pans swung and a collective groan went up as Charlie's heart sank lower than the feather.

The monster who waited by the scales slavered and capered in joyful anticipation. It licked its dripping jaws and opened wide.

Osiris frowned at Charlie and picked his heart up out of the balance pan. It rattled loudly. "Odd," the god said, and shook it. A pair of bullets dropped out of the heart and into Osiris's hand.

"Forgive me, my lord Osiris," the heart said. "May I be weighed again, without the lead?" Charlie stared, shocked at this bit of insolence. *It's a dream,* he reminded himself. *Of course a heart can back-talk a god.*

Osiris smiled. "Cheeky. As a reward for your sheer bravery, I will weigh you again."

Anubis snarled and the monster laid down and whined when Osiris put the heart back into the balance pan. This time, the feather sank to the floor. The room cheered and the monster slunk away. Anubis vanished with his balance.

Osiris came to Charlie, bearing his heart. "You have a brave and kind heart, child." He tipped the organ back into Charlie's chest, just as painlessly as he had taken it. Charlie covered the place with one hand, trying to feel it beating again. He wanted to gasp, more out of shock than discomfort, but felt it would be showy.

Isis stood beside her husband and took the bullets from his hand. "These have caused you great pain, child. But there is one who has rendered us a service and is in even greater pain from them. We will see to it that he need not endure such pain again."

She closed her hand and light flashed between her fingers. When she opened it again, a golden cartouche lay there. The hieroglyphics were of lead. She hung it about Charlie's neck, the fine gold chain contracting as she put it on until it hung just below the hollow of his throat.

Charlie bowed. "Thank you, great Isis."

"It reads, 'beloved son of Isis and Osiris.' As long as you wear it, you cannot die. It cannot be removed, except by force. If it ever is, child, you will return here to us to feast for eternity."

Osiris laid a gentle hand on his head. "You have helped break the curse that bound Khnum's children, the right man in the right place to aid them in making their apologies. Go in peace, with our love."

Charlie saw one of the other gods, a man with the head of a ram, lift a cup to him and then the banquet was receding, or he was being thrust away by a mighty force. Down he plunged into the night, stars rushing past him as he fell; down to the desert until he slammed into his own body.

He blinked his eyes open and saw nothing. He couldn't move; something bound him all around. He fought for breath and squirmed against the bindings. For a panicky moment, he thought Edward had mummified him. He worked one side free and uwrapped, and then he realized it was only the blanket, the same one they had made love on, and he'd been bundled in it to be taken back to Cairo.

He sat up and saw Edward packing. Although his lover's back was turned, he could hear the soft sobs.

"Edward," Charlie asked, softly, so as not to alarm him, "what have you done with my clothes?"

The soft voice didn't work. Edward nearly jumped out of his skin at the words and whirled with a terrified look on his handsome face.

"Please, love," Charlie said, "I'm naked. There's sand getting into uncomfortable places."

"You're dead," Edward said bluntly. "I'm going mad with grief," he muttered.

Charlie decided he had two options. He could keep telling himself it had all been a dream, or he could accept it all, now that it was over. The warming gold at his throat told him that if he wanted to keep any grip on reality at all, he had best opt for the latter. He decided to tell Edward everything, mad as it might sound.

"Yeah. I was dead. Osiris sent me back. The guys," Charlie nodded at the painting where Ni-ankh-khnum and Khnum-ho-tep still welcomed visitors into the tomb "put in a good word for me." As Edward looked between him and the painting, disbelief written on every line of his face, Charlie tapped the necklace. "Do you read hieroglyphics?"

"No." Edward approached him warily. "You didn't have that before."

"Isis gave it to me." Seeing his lover's caution, Charlie smiled. "I'm not a ghost or ghoul, not an evil spirit given your lover's shape. I'm just your Charles. I don't bite, Edward. Unless, of course, you ask."

Edward put out a careful finger and poked Charlie in the shoulder. Charlie covered his hand and used the other hand to pull him down for a kiss. Edward, believing at last, crushed Charlie to his chest and kissed him fiercely.

"I love you," Charlie said and bumped noses with him. Edward held him at arm's length and stared, his eyes wide, his mouth simultaneously trying to laugh and cry, then crushed him in again, tears flowing. Charlie caught one tear and kissed another.

"I thought I'd lost you." Edward kissed Charlie again, plunging deep to taste him, trying to make sure he was real.

"I was lost. Just out in the blackness and then I woke up in the tomb and found the manicurists and…" Charlie trailed off, aware that Edward was looking at him as if he'd lost his mind.

Edward ran gentle fingers over the bullet scar on his chest and the one on his back. "Closed, as they would look a year from now. And you're alive." He held Charlie's face in his hands and kissed him again. "I don't care about the rest, or how it happened. I have you."

Charlie smiled. "I'm a thank-you gift from Isis and Osiris. We were in the right place to help lift the curse."

"Curse?" Edward interrupted.

"Oh yeah, you weren't with me. That's Ni-ankh-khnum and Khnum-ho-tep there on the wall. They're devotees of Khnum the potter god and got caught in a competition between him and Osiris. Long story short, they made both the gods mad and got stuck here as spirits. They borrowed our bodies and made several kinds of apologies to Khnum." Charlie looked at the ground. "Including sex."

Edward blinked, showing he did remember but was fuzzy on what had happened before they had awakened. Charlie hurried on, condensing the tale.

"I had a couple adventures in the Land of the Dead, including a bath and a very thorough shave. They're really nice guys, a lot like us. Ni-ankh-khnum is a little envious though, of you and of the fact you get me."

"Is he now?" Edward looked a bit smug. "Did he say that?"

Charlie nodded. "Yeah." He slipped a hand down Edward's stomach and cupped his quiescent crotch. "You're better built."

"What else did they say?" Edward's tone said he was humoring Charlie, but Charlie didn't care. He told Edward everything he could remember of his adventure in the Land of the Dead, from the feast to the bath, the staircase of sky and the banquet of the gods, even the Balance.

Edward ran a hand over Charlie's bare armpit. "They shaved you, you said."

"Uh, yeah." Charlie turned to look and glanced down. "I didn't expect it to carry over." He suddenly felt much more naked than he had a moment ago. "My clothes?"

Edward yanked the pack over and dug out Charlie's clothes. "I didn't have the heart to try dressing your corpse." Charlie stood up and saw Edward's eyes go wide at the sight of his hairless body. Edward handed over the clothes, still staring. "At least they didn't get bloody," he mumbled. He reached out and touched one finger to the bare skin of Charlie's groin.

"Elsewhere, please," Charlie said, wanting more, but having the strong feeling he shouldn't. "It feels a bit disrespectful right here. And if you keep touching me like that, I'm going to have to kiss you more and we'll end up both naked in the sand. Which isn't at all comfortable." He dusted away sand as he pulled up his pants.

Edward's face had lost much of its grief-stricken look, replacing it with desire tinged with lust. "That's just how we started. But, I quite agree it's time to be on our way." He finished the packing and reached for one of the bracelets that lay on the table in the banqueting chamber.

Charlie, still struggling into his boots, stopped him. "Lord Osiris made me swear I had not stolen the food of the dead. That means we shouldn't be taking their things either. Besides, that's Khnum-ho-tep's favorite." He paused, listening to a voice that Edward could not hear. "They say there is a small cache of ornaments intended for their servants in the burial chamber. It is our reward for helping them."

Charlie led the way and opened a panel in the stone wall. The voice told him where to find it and how to open it. Edward just shook his head, disbelief all over his features. From inside the panel, Charlie pulled three alabaster boxes, larger than a man's hand. He lifted the lid off of one. Gold and sapphires gleamed in earrings and bracelets. Gold bells adorned another bracelet.

"Better than one bracelet?" Charlie handed the boxes to Edward and finished putting himself in order. "Now, sir, I believe something was said about going back to Cairo?"

Edward added the boxes to their pack, wrapping them carefully in the unstained parts of the blanket to protect the fragile stones.

"Oh, yes. Do hurry, Charles." He shouldered the pack.

Charlie picked up the saddlebags and paused a moment to pour out two handfuls of water in front of the banquet painting. "Thank you, guys." He touched the picture of the manicurists gently and then followed Edward out of the tomb.

Night had fallen here as well when the sandstorm abated. Their horses were nowhere to be found and it was a thirty-mile walk back to Cairo. They shouldered their packs and started the trudge.

Out of Saqqara, they fell in with a caravan of traders headed for the city to be at the bazaar by dawn. A few piastres bought a spot in an oxcart. The caravan moved no faster than they could have walked, but Charlie was grateful to lie down, Edward beside him on the bundles of straw, watching the stars turn and grow dim as the night grew old. They talked of everything except the tomb. Charlie dragged out all the old myths he knew about constellations for Edward's amusement. They hatched and discarded wild plans for getting Sir Alex's body back. Charlie dozed for a while, exhausted by the day's excitement, but the cart's motion prevented him from sleeping deeply.

They arrived at the hotel just after dawn, tired and hungry, the water-skins empty. From the harbor, they heard the long honk of the steamship before it pulled away from the quay. Edward slumped into a chair in their room, as defeated-looking as Charlie had ever seen him.

"That's it then. They're headed back with Sir Alex's body. The adventure is over. Let's recover before we head back to England. There's no more need for haste."

"Are you sure? Is there no way to catch up?"

"None. The steamer left. And any other route will take several days."

"I'm sorry, my lord. I didn't expect to be dead for so long." Charlie flung himself on the bed. "What I wouldn't give for a cup of the beer they handed me." He looked up at Edward. "I didn't eat or drink over there."

"Wise choice, Charles." Edward handed him a fresh waterskin. "I'm too tired to coax anything edible out of the ration tins."

Charlie drank a little and sat up. "I can go down to the market."

"No dancing girls." Edward yawned, unlacing his boots and pulling Charlie into his embrace. "Just bread and some fruit if there's any good."

Charlie was asleep before he could ask for a sixpence to accomplish the shopping. He woke to red sunset. Edward was still sleeping. Charlie filched a handful of millemes from his employer's purse and left a note.

Charlie headed out to the street, Edward's snores following him down the steps. A shilling went a long way in Egypt, and Charlie returned to the room with almost more food than he could carry. He ate a few grapes and tumbled into bed beside Edward for another nap.

They slept the evening and half the night away, and Charlie woke again when the moon shone high and bright. He kindled a lantern, had a quick wash, and arranged the fruit and bread on a platter. He opened a tin of the apple and red plum jam that was Edward's favorite. Then he stripped and wrapped a spare sheet around his waist, approximating the skirt the manicurists had put him in. He regretted he didn't think to buy kohl in the market.

Edward was lying perfectly still in the bed, curled into a tight ball. His eyes moved under the closed lids and his breathing came fast. Charlie laid one hand on his forehead to see if he was getting feverish again. They didn't need a malaria relapse.

Edward sat bolt upright, grasping Charlie's wrist, and shouting questions at him in what sounded like German.

"Edward, you're hurting," Charlie said.

A solid backhand with Edward's free hand rattled Charlie's teeth and made him forget the pain in his wrist. He pulled away and stood up. "Edward!" he yelled. The next step would be a blow of his own if Edward didn't wake.

Edward fell back to the bed and stirred.

"Edward, do wake up. You're worrying me," he said, sitting on the edge of the bed. "Wake up and see what a breakfast I've got for you." Charlie rubbed his aching jaw. Edward was a big man and packed a wallop.

"Is it Monday?" Edward mumbled, batting at Charlie to make him quit pestering. Charlie stayed well out of reach.

"I have no idea. It's night again, but almost dawn. And how long was I dead?" Charlie asked, tipping Edward's face around for a kiss.

Edward opened his eyes, smiled, and blinked a little at Charlie. "I don't remember," he said, looking sheepish. "Hours at least. We found the tomb about noon and you didn't wake up until dark." He pulled Charlie down for a kiss. Charlie winced at the pain in his face.

"What's wrong?"

"You hit me. You were having a really bad nightmare or something. I thought it might be malaria. You grabbed me, questioned me in German, and hit me."

Edward sighed. "Well, damn. It's a good stretch, and I'm sorry it's over." He pulled Charlie's face closer and examined the red mark that would shortly become a bruise. "Are you all right? I'm very sorry about this."

"I'll be fine. What happened?"

"War nightmare. I have four recurring ones. Happens most often when I'm under stress. It sounds like you tried waking me from *Down Behind Enemy Lines*. That's the worst one."

"We've definitely had some stress recently. You've named your nightmares?" Charlie reached for his notebook.

"They're easier to recover from if I think of them as terrible cinema. There's *Down Behind Enemy Lines*. I've been shot down and am trying to get back to our side. I am spotted and have to capture and interrogate the German soldier who sees me." Charlie wrote fast, taking down everything Edward told him. This was important and he knew he would use it in the future.

"You shouldn't try waking me from that one. I nearly killed Nigel once when he did. Let it run its course, and I will wake. *Archie* is about flying at night, which is lovely until the anti-aircraft fire shoots me down. Some nights it's a nice clean crash, others it's a nasty walking hit and I take bullets as well as the plane. Feel free to wake me as soon as you realize that one. *The Red Baron* involves me dogfighting that worthy. It's safe to wake me from that, and if you can do so before he shoots me down, all the better." Edward gave Charlie a wan smile. "I wake up better if I haven't been strewn all over the landscape. The last, *Aerodrome*, isn't nearly so clear cut. I'm back in the aerodrome, and I'm looking for something. I can't find it, and I won't stop looking, even though we're being bombed. Wake me from that one as quickly as you can."

"Yes, sir." Charlie brought the food over and changed the subject. "We had quite a journey last night. Have something to eat." Charlie cut a strip of melon and fed it to him. He took some of the pinkish orange flesh for himself and enjoyed the sweetness. He offered some bread with jam and pomegranate seeds sprinkled on it.

"I'm starved." Edward sat up and helped himself to more bread and some olives and dates. "Thank you, Charles. Did you get enough sleep?"

"Plenty. I just woke up a few minutes ago."

Edward had just broken open a fig, when he stopped and looked at Charlie. "What are you wearing?"

Charlie looked down, as if noticing his clothes for the first time. "Sorry. It felt more real than my clothes did this morning."

Edward looked a little more. "It's... I like it."

"It's comfortable. And suited to the climate." Charlie ate some more grapes and tried the dates.

Edward set the end of the fig aside and patted his lap. "Come here." He pulled Charlie to stand between his legs and stroked the smooth, compact body. "We have lost a day and a night recovering. I'll see if I can get a rail schedule and get us on the earliest train to England." He sounded thoroughly defeated and unhappy. "We've lost, Charles. It's time to go home. But I think we can spare your stomach the Mediterranean."

"Thank you." Charlie bent in and bumped noses with him.

Edward laughed. "Are you going to keep doing that?"

"I don't know. Are we going to talk about what happened yesterday?" Charlie pressed a little closer into Edward. "I'd like it to happen again. When we're both present. And back home."

"Charles, I-" Edward paused. "I have no idea what actually happened yesterday. We took refuge in a tomb, found Sir Alex, and then, I don't remember anything until Sarah showed up and we were in flagrante. Nigel shot you, and I fear I did too. You died, they took the other body and left me with yours. I lost all sense of time. Finally, I started packing for the trip back, not knowing how I wold explain to your parents. You came back to life and saved me that part."

"Yeah, that's pretty much it. I came back from the possession before you did. You were still Ni-ankh-khnum and still making love to me when I started being Charlie again. I liked it. I liked the feeling of your body, the little noises you make."

Edward looked abashed. "I'm quite disappointed that I wasn't present."

Charlie tucked his head into Edward's shoulder, kissing his neck and jaw. "It's all right. I love you," he said softly.

Edward gripped him more firmly. "Love you, Charles. And I will be there for the next."

Charlie stepped out of the embrace and looked at the skirt. "I'll put on some real clothes and pack, you go find the schedule and let's get out of here."

# CHAPTER 7

# BACK ON THE ROAD

**Unwilling** to subject me to another Trial by Boat, Lord Withycombe arranged a much longer journey overland to spare my insides. I don't believe I ever thanked him properly, but even almost a week on a creaky train between Cairo and Constantinople was preferable to three days on the water.

—From the journal of Charles Doyle, secretary to Lord Withycombe

*****

They packed what was needed from the little place and left, boarding the northern train from Cairo through the British Mandate of Palestine and the Emirate of Transjordan to the nascent Republic of Turkey.

From Cairo, they traveled to Amman, Jordan. Charlie spent much of the trip watching out the window as the lush river valley gave way to the barren Sinai peninsula, with its rugged crags and peaks. He was astounded to see the lands his grandmother and mother had talked about all of his boyhood coming to life before his eyes. He shut his eyes and tried to imagine what one of the stunted bushes would look like, burning and not consuming itself. But all he could see was Isis's smile.

In Amman, Edward handed Charlie a pile of clothing. Charlie looked at the loose trousers, the high-collared tunic with embroidery, and the burnoose.

140

"Transjordan is not entirely secure. We will travel in greater safety if we dress as locals, Charles." Edward had already changed and was winding a turban around a small fez with a fast and practiced hand. Charlie watched, enraptured at his skill.

"You look—"

"Dress," Edward ordered. Charlie pulled the strange clothes on over his own at once. Edward nodded at the look of him and set a fez on his head. "Go about your business."

Charlie understood then that they were in danger again. He settled himself down, took out his typewriter and wrote for a while. Edward settled next to him, smoking a foul little black cigarette and speaking to no one.

When a group of men came aboard, Charlie typed harder, determined to make so much racket they wouldn't stay in the car. Five of them moved on, but one sat in the back of the car. Charlie kept writing, not caring what he put on the paper about Paris and the French girl, Osiris and the manicurists, or even the way Edward had hit him during the nightmare.

Charlie could feel Edward almost vibrating with tension. The presence of the man in the car weighed on his mind. He typed harder and faster, talking about how Edward looked in his native garb. This segued into a distinctly erotic fantasy about Edward as a desert raider, kidnapping him from a train platform and hauling him into the desert to alternately feed him dates and flat bread and ravish him beneath bright stars. The fantasy helped ease his mind a little.

A large gloved hand came down on Charlie's typewriter. He stared at the gold jackal-headed ring over the leather. "There are other travelers. Be considerate with your racket," the man from the last row growled at him in accented English, his voice as rusty as an old gate. "Your clothes fool no one."

Edward glared up at the intruder and removed the man's hand from the machine. Charlie rolled the paper up without a word and blushed to see what he'd typed. He hastily put his paper away and reached for the lid of the case. There was no sense in making a follower of Anubis angry. He hadn't liked the way the Death God had looked at him back in Osiris's feasting chamber.

When he closed the typewriter, Edward handed him his journal and pen, silently. Charlie nodded. The man nodded. "Stay silent." He returned to his post.

Edward did stay silent. They rode through the night, Edward snoring with his burnoose hood pulled down over his face. Charlie dozed against the window. In brief wakings, he realized the snore pattern was all wrong and knew Edward was keeping watch.

They pulled into Constantinople in the wee hours of the morning and Charlie yawned as he carried his case and carpetbag to the platform. Edward breathed more easily when the men went the other direction and climbed into a cab.

"We're going to take a ferry across to Sirkeci terminal on the European side. The Orient Express will take us back to Paris."

Charlie rolled his eyes. "Another boat."

"You did well on the train." Edward patted his shoulder. "Cheer up, we could be taking the route that requires a ferry clear to Varna."

The ferry wasn't terrible. The water was fairly smooth and he wasn't on it more than an hour. Some strong Turkish tea fortified him and he sat comfortably until they docked on the Europe side of Turkey.

His cheer vanished when they reached the Sirkeci terminal. The train had left at the usual twenty-two hundred and the next one did not leave until the following night. The clerk telephoned the Pera Palas

Hotel, the one attached to the rail company, and found them the last room in the place. Edward frowned again when told it was a single.

"I'll make do, sir," Charlie said, yawning hugely. "Prop me in a corner or something."

As they waited for the promised cab in the foyer, Edward leaned down and whispered, "It could be fun sharing a single bed."

"Not awake, sir, just sleepwalking. And you haven't slept since Cairo, not really." Charlie loaded his baggage when the cab arrived and dozed during the short drive to the hotel. He was glad the entrance was at street level and promised himself he'd remember the approach to the massive building in the morning.

Even the high-arching foyer, done in the original Victorian style, couldn't wake Charlie enough to do more than glance at the domed skylights and large wood doors. He would explore tomorrow.

"We cannot afford this, pleasant as it will be," Edward mumbled when he saw the luxurious room, the curtains covering tall windows that looked out over Constantinople. "Doesn't matter. I'll make my banker afford it." He stripped to his underwear and stretched out on the wide brass bed and beckoned Charlie.

Charlie stripped and lay down beside him. "Their single's big enough for a double," he mumbled. He kissed Edward's neck, settled into his shoulder, and went straight back to sleep.

*****

Charlie woke late to Edward snoring beside him and his own stomach rumbling. He slipped out to the water closet. Charlie stared briefly at the hot water faucet, a luxury even in New York. He couldn't imagine what the room would cost here in Turkey. Then he returned to kiss Edward awake.

When he came up for air, he saw the faintest gleam of hazel eye between Lord Edward's closed lashes and knew his lover was faking sleep. Scrapping the kissing plan, he bounced on the edge of the bed, working at Edward's underwear.

"Edward. Get up. Up, my lord. Please, Edward, wake up." He bounced on every "up." "I want to-" He had no idea what he'd planned to say he wanted to do because Edward seized him, cutting him off, and kissed him hard.

"Good morning." Edward smiled as he rolled Charlie underneath him. "What was that you wanted to do again?"

"Take up where we never quite got started in Egypt?" Charlie kissed him. "And then explore the hotel. Eat and explore some more." He traced his hand down Edward's chest.

The maid chose that moment to knock at the door. Both of them looked at it in panic. In Turkish and Greek, followed by French, she announced they would need to leave so she could clean the room. "Unless, the gentlemen are staying tonight as well?" she added.

"We're staying over," Edward called back. The maid acknowledged them and moved on.

Charlie mimed wiping sweat from his face and pulled Edward down for another kiss. "I'm game for anything else you want to do. It's closer to noon, though and I'm hungry. So let's make it fast."

"Brave lad. I think I would prefer to linger a bit the first time." Edward rolled them out of the bed. "Besides, you said you were hungry and I can't bear to look at another tin. There will be time in England for everything we want." He kissed Charlie again, very thoroughly.

Charlie understood that delayed gratification was not a hallmark of Edward's personality. For him to put off their lovemaking, especially in the name of safety. was uncharacteristic and wiser than Charlie expected. But it didn't alleviate his frustration. He wanted so much more than just kisses and sleeping in Edward's arms.

Charlie nodded. "Lunch, my lord and love?"

Edward tossed him a damp cloth. "Western clothing, please, dear." He wiped himself clean, washing away the dust of traveling, and dressed to his waist, letting his suspenders hang. "Charles, love, do you mind shaving me?" he asked as he circled the brush in the shaving mug. "You do it so sweetly."

Charlie washed up as Edward lathered his face. "Of course." He tied a towel around his waist and took up the razor. After stropping it on the back of his belt, he stroked it over Edward's jaw. "I enjoy shaving you. It's intimate. Personal, you know?"

Edward neither nodded nor smiled, but his soft sigh as Charlie ran the razor over his face said more than either. Charlie scraped the suds away, patted him down with a towel and tested the closeness by kissing the smooth skin.

He checked himself hastily, found no need to shave, and so cleaned up the equipment before getting dressed. When everything was packed, he handed Edward his pipe, tobacco, and matches.

"Charles, love, you think of everything." He took the tobacco and began loading his pipe. "Now, how to kill the hours before our train arrives? We seem to have an abundance of them."

"Lunch would be swell, sir." Charlie reminded him. "We didn't eat much but apples and bread on the train and I'm really hungry."

"The market then." Edward checked his wallet and Charlie checked his purse.

"If we can find a buyer, we shouldn't have to worry." Charlie held up the golden pot necklace that

Safi had left when she went up in smoke. "The guys won't mind."

"Clever boy. An honest dealer will give us enough for the room and the train and your lunch, even if you decide to devour a whole ox."

"Mmm," Charlie said as they headed out. "Ox burger, ox steak, oxtail soup, a nice stew, some pan-fried liver and onions."

"Oh hush, Charles. Eyes bigger than your stomach."

Making sure they were alone in the hall, Charlie grinned. "That's what Ni-ankh-khnum said too."

*****

Discreet inquiries of the desk clerk led them to a little shop in a shifty looking quarter of the city. The sign creaked as if about to fall from its hinges. Edward laid the necklace on the counter and let the jeweler examine it.

"I only want to know its value," he said in French.

"Speak English," the jeweler said, his English accented with Greek. "Your schoolbook words reek with the accent of the gutters and brothels."

Edward gave Charlie a half-smile. "It was my mother's and we find ourselves in desperate straits."

"Englishmen," the old Greek man grumbled. "You all lie like dogs." He turned the little necklace over in his hand, feeling the gold pendant and testing the chain. "It is gold, at least." He named a figure far too low.

Charlie, hungry and sick of the Eastern custom of haggling over every price, slapped a hand on the counter. He cursed the clerk's ancestry, hygiene, and sexual practices in the harsh mix of Arabic and English that he'd picked up in Cairo. For good measure, he added, "Your wife smells like a goat and your daughter is too ugly to marry even with a bag over her head!" From the corner of his eye, he saw Edward stifle a smile and hide his sneeze that had started as a laugh, but he remained leaning over the counter, his face near the jeweler's face, his nostrils flared, his eyes wide and a snarl that showed too many teeth on his face. "Now give us a fair price, you thief who steals the carrion with the vultures still inside it!" Charlie demanded.

The jeweler laughed. "You have been bargaining with Egyptians, boy. I like you." He looked at the piece more closely. "For you, I will make a good bargain. I do it because you are pretty and because your lover is a small man, in many ways."

The shopkeeper stole a glance at Edward's crotch and Charlie was pretty sure that had been meant as an insult, both the statement that they were lovers and Edward's endowment. The jeweler named a figure that would more than cover the room and the ticket, meals, and some lodging in Paris.

"It is older than that, you thief. You steal milk out of the mouths of babes and coins from the eyes of the dead. They curse your name as they wander the banks of the Styx, unable to pay Charon to take them across." Charlie was soaring free now, unfettered by haggling tradition or good taste. He doubled the amount the man offered.

The jeweler wailed. "Oh, the foreign infidels, bankrupting me, stealing my daughter's dowry. She is indeed very ugly and I need all I can scrape. Now she will marry the ragpicker, for your English greed!" He counted out the price he had offered in a mixture of currencies from drachmae to francs and pounds and added another ten pounds. "That is all, all. You rob me."

Charlie pocketed the cash. "A thousand blessings and good fortune and a rich and handsome suitor for your daughter, most noble of jewelers." He shook hands with the jeweler, who was smiling broadly.

As they left, Edward shook his head. "I didn't know you had all that in you. Most impressive."

Charlie grinned. "I'm the one who had to go find dinner with a shilling in my pocket. And I picked up a little from working with Dad. Some of the old Italian men who come to him think haggling for the price is as much fun as getting a new suit. They laughed at the stupid Irishman who couldn't argue like they do." Charlie's look grew fierce. "They never laughed at me."

"One more reason to be glad I chose you." Edward led the way back to the hotel and they settled the bill and bought their tickets. "We'll be taking the Arlberg Orient Express. Lovely. Some of the best scenery in the world."

"Meals are included in the price, but drinks are extra," Charlie read from the ticket. The difference in names of the trains meant nothing to him. "Well, that's good. Because those tickets put a serious dent in the bankroll."

"Yes, but in three luxurious days we'll be in Paris, sipping champagne and enjoying the favors of your pretty can-can girl." Edward settled into a lobby sofa for a smoke. "Such a pity we didn't invite the maid in this morning."

Charlie sat down and took out his notebook. He recorded selling the necklace, made a small K in the corner to remember the kisses and speculated about the Orient Express.

They lazed the afternoon away, sipping drinks in the hotel bar and finally at five, they changed for dinner. The dining car wouldn't be attached to the train until the next morning, just in time for breakfast.

# CHAPTER 8

# THE ORIENT EXPRESS

The heat of battle is said to be a thrilling thing, full of wild charges and glory. No, it's much more a deal of confusion, some small action, and the inevitable moment of wondering what in the blazes just happened.

—From the journal of Charles Doyle, secretary to Lord Withycombe

*****

Charlie stared at the four blue and gold coaches and two baggage vans that comprised the legendary Orient Express. He carried his typewriter into the little double sleeping compartment himself. Edward tipped their porter and Charlie made himself comfortable on the chintz seat.

"I thought it'd be bigger," he said. Realizing he sounded ungrateful, he added, "The compartment's nice and roomy, but I thought the train would be longer."

Edward shook his head. "Very exclusive accommodations, Charles. It will be longer when they add the dining car tomorrow." Slowly, the train chuffed out of the station, gradually picking up speed.

Charlie watched the Greek night fly past them and scribbled in his notebook for a while. Then the porter knocked.

"Would the gentlemen like their beds turned down?" he asked. Edward nodded and led Charlie out to the water closet. Even this was spotlessly clean, in contrast to some of the more nightmarish train toilets Charlie had seen. Charlie brushed his teeth and changed into Edward's spare nightshirt. Despite London, Paris and Cairo, he still hadn't had an opportunity to replace his own. Besides, he had grown attached to Edward's.

"We'll see a lot of the porter. He's assigned to our compartment," Edward explained. "And why aren't you wearing your own pajamas, Charles?"

Charlie looked sheepish. "I like sleeping in yours. And I still haven't found any."

"It does make you look delectable." Edward opened the door to the compartment. Their porter had lowered a top bunk out of the wall and folded the seat into a lower one. Both of them looked inviting with crisp white sheets and plump pillows. "I'll take the bottom bunk. Should yours send you crashing into me in the night, I'm sure I should survive. I'm less sanguine about the reverse."

The train hit a bump in the rails and Charlie, seeing a moment, lunged into Edward's arms. "I'm sorry, sir," he said, hiding his smile behind a look of overdone contrition, "I didn't mean to crash into you."

Edward set him on his feet. "You must spend some small portion of the night in your bed, Charles."

Charlie climbed up, allowing Edward a good look under the nightshirt. "Yes, sir."

Edward turned off the compartment lights and settled into his own bed. "I did say a small portion, my dear. Muss the berth a bit and then come down here."

Charlie obeyed that order quite happily.

*****

Charlie woke in the middle of the night when the train stopped to couple new cars and climbed back into the top bunk. At eight, Constantinople time, their porter came around with breakfast.

Edward was already up and dressed. Charlie sat up and yawned, grabbing for a dressing gown. He climbed down and let the porter turn his bunk back to a banquette. They dressed for breakfast, Charlie deciding the occasion called for his good suit and a tie. Edward just smiled and pushed Charlie's glasses up where they belonged.

A few minutes later, a waiter arrived with their breakfast. Edward uncovered the tray and beamed. The smell of good coffee made Charlie smile.

"Finally, true civilization." He poured out the coffee and sat down to porridge and bacon, eggs and sausage, and toast with jam. Charlie joined him and stared out the window at the scenery. "Isn't that lovely?" Edward drank more coffee and admired the view of the mountains.

"Gorgeous. I've never seen anything like it. I'm a city boy, with only side trips to my grandma's farm."

"I knocked around Europe for years before and after the war. Backpacked, hitchhiked, slummed." Edward drank the end of the coffee. Charlie set the demolished breakfast tray outside for their porter and settled into his seat, just watching the landscape.

Edward cleared his throat and Charlie snapped back to attention. "Charles," he began.

Charlie rose smoothly. In a trice, he returned with Edward's pipe, tobacco, and matches, as well as his own notebook. Edward smiled and started his pipe going.

"I couldn't bear being home," Edward went on. "I lost both of my parents while I was fighting in France. My father passed from his weak heart and my mother from her own broken one shortly afterward."

Charlie made sympathetic noises and took furious notes. He added the marginal note, "biography," and kept writing.

"So I traveled, largely on credit. And I healed slowly. People must have thought it all quite exotic, for when I got home I had a reputation as an adventurer." He smiled at Charlie and puffed thoughtfully. "General Elizabeth kept my household running while I was away. The trust my father created saw to it that everything was taken care of, wages and repairs and such like. Since I already had the adventurous reputation, I decided to put it to work for me. I became a specialist in retrieving lost artifacts or people. It turned out I needed that employ when a great many letters of credit came due. I understand several of our ancestral lands in Cambridgeshire were sold to cover my wastrel years." He finished the pipe and set it aside. Charlie missed the warm smell of burning tobacco. "The lands I didn't mind so much. I'm no farmer. But the verbal thrashing from my banker, that set me back a bit."

Charlie wrote quickly, frowning at the tale. Edward leaned across the gap in the seats and stroked the line the frown made between his eyebrows.

"My greatest difficulty has been loneliness. It is difficult to find a companion willing to travel as I do and make himself useful." He came to sit beside Charlie and patted his knee. "But I've fixed that now."

Charlie looked up and smiled. "I'm glad. I'm looking forward to new adventures."

"We aren't done with this one yet."

The short hairs on the back of Charlie's neck tingled. He'd been extra alert since the time in the Land of the Dead, all his senses seeming to register more than usual. This time, something told him danger was incoming.

"You're right. Get down." He didn't know why he said it, but it seemed the right thing at that time and he dove for the floor.

Edward's combat reflexes sent him down atop Charlie. Something large smashed through the window of the moving train, spattering them with glass.

Charlie looked up to see Edward was back on his feet. He stayed down, fitting himself into the corner of the train compartment. The projectile turned out to be a man, of a sort. It looked dead, long dead, its skin gray and shriveled like the rot Safi had left on Charlie back in Cairo. It moved creakily, each motion exuding a smell of rotten spices and wilted chrysanthemums. But the hooked knife in its hand gleamed wickedly.

Charlie curled into as small a ball as he could so that Edward would have room to fight. The knife slashed down but Edward dodged handily, the knife missing him and shredding one of the seat covers.

Edward gripped the thing's arm and slammed it against the paneled wall of the compartment. The flesh powdered away in a puff of gray dust and the bone shattered. The knife fell to the floor. Edward battered the creature's head against the wall and finally got hold of its collar. Charlie watched as Edward gave the walking corpse the bum's rush, as if it were an ordinary drunk and not a supernatural creature, hurling him back out the window. Together they watched it bounce down the slight slope, bashing into trees and breaking apart in bursts of desiccated flesh.

Edward swept the car with his eyes, clearly expecting more attackers. Charlie felt his rapid breathing start to slow. Now that they were safe again, the mess the thing had made of their compartment worried him. "I'll get the porter to see to the glass and the seat, shall I?"

"Yes, thank you, Charles."

The porter was most accommodating when they explained about the large bird that had smashed through the window and moved them to a new compartment at once. The train was half empty, so there was no inconvenience.

Charlie gathered up their things and they made themselves at home in the new compartment, but the joy of the trip was gone. Something was out there, waiting for them. Charlie could feel it in his short neck hairs, a low crawling sensation. It was the same sensation the robed man on the train had given him. Politics of the volatile region they had just left had been dangerous enough. Supernatural attackers would have only complicated their trip more. He hoped the new senses would help.

The porter came by after they'd settled to tell them lunch was served and to deliver a ring. "I thought you might have forgotten it, sir," he said, handing it to Charlie.

Charlie looked at the golden jackal's head, the same one he had seen on the train in Jordan, its black enameling peeling with age. "Yes, thank you." He shut the door and folded the cartouche at his throat into one hand, letting the edges cut into him, feeling the hieroglyphics print themselves on his palm, as he reminded himself that Isis and Osiris loved him. The solution to the mystery of the attack came to him, soft as a feather from Isis' headdress.

"Charles? What do you have?" Edward peered over his shoulder.

"A warning from Anubis." Charlie made himself let go of the pendant and opened the other hand to show the ring. "He's angry that I freed Khnum's men from the half-place he had consigned them to. Khnum is pleased with me, but Anubis... I don't know how I feel about having a god unhappy with me."

"Charles…" Edward laid a hand on his forehead. "Were you bitten by a mosquito? Have you hit your head? You're not making much sense."

"Sense? Edward, you just fought a man dead for hundreds of years. You torched a dead girl who tried to seduce me. And you're going to strain at the gnat of Anubis while swallowing the camel of revived corpses?"

"A splendid point, my dear." He settled Charlie back in the seat and rang for the porter. When the porter returned with his order, he poured Charlie a cup of tea and added a healthy slug of brandy to it. He sipped at his own double whiskey.

Charlie sipped the tea, looking unnerved by both the attack and the revelation from the gods.

"I wonder how angry he is and how far his power extends. Can he follow us all the way to France?" Edward mused as he drank. His tone said he might not believe it but he wasn't looking forward to a repeat attack.

Charlie heard a voice, not quite his, saying, "The Lord of the Embalming Chamber is wherever people are dying."

"Then how do we appease him?"

Charlie shook his head, the oddness gone. He took a large drink of the tea. "He is unhappy because I robbed him three times. Of the manicurists and of myself." He closed his hand over the cartouche again, seeming to feel Isis's comforting wings fold about him.

"So three deaths should appease him, then," Edward suggested. "But who to kill?"

"I have three in mind," Charlie said, a sickly but wicked grin on his face. It faded. "But I swore to Lord Osiris I hadn't killed."

"Charles," Edward looked stern, then relaxed. "That's an oath I'm pleased you were able to take. I should like you to keep it. I couldn't say the same, I fear."

Charlie drank the end of his tea and felt fortified by the brandy in it. "Well, we handled the first hunter well enough. It's not as if you don't have enemies, already. We'll just have to be on the lookout for more." He took his teacup and the empty whiskey glass and set them outside the door, then locked it behind him. He settled on the same seat as Edward and curled into his employer's side.

Edward said nothing, but wrapped an arm around Charlie. They sat together as the sweet spring afternoon faded into dusk. They dressed for dinner and ate in the dining car, enjoying the tender pheasant that swam luxuriously in its tangy elderberry sauce.

They ate quietly, neither wanting to say much about the excitement. Charlie obligingly mussed his bunk and then crawled into Edward's, desperate for more touch, for the reassurance he was indeed alive.

Edward gave all the comfort he wanted. The warm smell of whiskey and tobacco and the lingering elderberries from dinner all blended with Edward's own scent to make Charlie very aware that it was not solely comfort he had come down for.

He kissed the side of Edward's neck. "I love you," he said, his voice soft in the dark. Charlie held his breath, waiting for Edward's response.

"Do you, darling?" Edward asked, equally softly. Charlie nodded. "Shall we say enough of the three month trial and let you stay on permanently, then?"

"Yes? Please?" Charlie looked up at him. "I don't think I could stand the idea of leaving after three months."

"Neither can I."

"But, on one condition, Edward."

"Yes?"

"I pack for the next adventure."

Edward laughed. "Of course."

He tipped Charlie's face up and kissed him. Charlie melted into the kiss, pressing close along the length of Edward's body, his nightshirt suddenly a hindrance, a barrier to what he craved.

When Edward let go, Charlie sat up and stripped out of the nightshirt, then lay back down beside him. "I'm crazy for wanting you after the day we had."

"Not at all," Edward reassured him. "Combat often leads to sex." He ran a lingering hand over Charlie's side, leaving a little trail of sparks in Charlie's skin. "Believe me, I know. Best put the nightshirt back on. We're not taking chances, Charles. Anything could happen and I shouldn't want us to be taken by surprise and en flagrante. Again."

Charlie popped the nightshirt back over his head and curled back into Edward's arms. "Tell me," he whispered.

"It's really the only thing that makes extended combat bearable." Edward stroked his face. Charlie just buried his face in Edward's shoulder and let him touch, the big hands gentle on his back and arms, and talk. The low whispers were things he could never put in a biography. "Flight helps. But a lover helps more. Knowing that when you get back to the base… if you get back, he'll be there. And you have one more night."

"Every night," Charlie whispered, back. "I'll be there every night."

"Every. Single. One." Edward punctuated his words with three taps of Charlie's nose and kissed him again, long and slow.

That was when all hell broke loose.

Charlie would later write the story in a pulp fiction novel, but even then he knew he would have to leave out salient details. The book claimed they were both in asleep. It was most embarrassing to have five of the dead men burst through their door with them distracted by Edward's tongue in his mouth and hands on his body.

Edward, less distracted, rolled Charlie beneath him and sprang out of the bunk. Charlie had enough presence of mind to get up and put the compartment window down.

The little room reeked of embalming spices and dead flowers as the revenants jockeyed for position. Edward yanked the first into the room and hurled it out the window Charlie had just gotten open.

"Rather tiresome, this lot. Did he break adequately?" Edward said as he threw another in Charlie's direction and ducked the knives of the other three.

"All to pieces, sir," Charlie said as he caught the man and heaved it out, aiming for some rocks. They were less terrifying this time around. Now that he knew how fragile they were, he felt up to the task of getting rid of them.

Edward got the third and threw it. The revenant hung up on the window and Charlie tipped it out, wincing as the train ran it over.

"At least they're brainless," Edward said, smashing the fourth one's arm to powder and taking its knife.

Charlie yelped as the fifth edged its way in and seized him by the back of the necklace. The dead man twisted the necklace, trying to break it. Charlie choked in the golden noose, Isis's gift of life turning into a deathtrap. He shoved himself backward, pounding them both against the wall and smearing mummy dust on the window. Charlie slammed his head back trying to smash the mummy's face.

The things couldn't be stunned. Charlie turned and flipped the nightmare over his head and out the window, its fingers breaking off in the chain. He heard the dusty crunch as it hit a tree. He fell to the floor coughing for air and dusting away the fingers and other dust. The last one sailed out, past his head, and Edward slammed the window shut before sinking to the floor beside him.

"Are you all right?" Edward asked, running a light finger around the chafing on Charlie's throat.

Without answering, Charlie flung himself on Edward, arms around his neck. He kissed his lover frantically, clumsy in his haste, covering the whole of Edward's mouth and face with kisses.

Edward laughed when Charlie let him go. "I suspect that's a yes." He lay down on the bunk and Charlie slid into his arms. Charlie got comfortable and let Edward stroke his hair until the tired hero drifted to sleep. Then Charlie rose, took his notebook and went to the salon car to write until he was tired.

He couldn't tell everything of course. No one would believe it as an addition to his biography of Edward. But it would make a splendid pulp novel. He sipped tea, writing diligently, recording all he could remember of the attacks. He closed his hand around the cartouche, this time in gratitude, not for reassurance. He felt calmness pervade him. The danger was past for now.

# CHAPTER 9

# BACK TO PARIS

Breakfasting on the Orient Express was a most pleasant experience. The whole trip remains in my mind as one of the most comfortable and luxurious journeys I ever enjoyed, at least after the defenestration of Anubis's men. The fine wood paneling, the green shaded lamps, the crisp linen turned down every night, and the elegant food all made me feel not only slightly out of place, but like the lord my employer was.

—From the journal of Charles Doyle, secretary to Lord Withycombe


*****


When they stepped off the Orient Express, it was with real regret on Charlie's part that this leg of their journey was over. Paris fluttered around them, blossoming with spring. He watched Edward appreciate the length of leg being shown by the French girls this season.

They checked into a fading hotel in Montmarte; fading, but not yet gone to seed. The room was clean and if the furniture was old, it was still solid. The maid set a cot in the corner of the room for Charlie and he opened his typewriter on the desk.

During the last two days of the train ride, he'd gotten more stories out of Edward. Now, Charlie rolled the paper into the machine in the interstices of listening to Edward grumble under his breath as he dictated yet another telegram to his London banker. Charlie had been privy to all the correspondence Edward sent—had edited most of it to ten words, in fact. But he didn't know what the London banker was saying that left his lord so cranky.

When Edward went downstairs to send it, Charlie started typing. He wanted to get the pulp story of the mummies and the train attack written. He might be able to get a few shillings from a London newspaper or find a publisher who would let him make it a serial.

Dreams of actual royalty payments dancing in his head, he clacked away, never hearing Edward come back in. He looked up when he smelled pipe smoke and found Edward watching him. He gave his lover a smile and finished the page.

"Are you ready for a break, Charles? You chain yourself to that infernal noisemaker with more enthusiasm than you eat. Which is saying a great deal."

Charlie sighed. "I managed a page. On the train I was doing six or eight a day." He looked up. "Might as well level with you. I'm writing pulp fiction. No one will believe the dancing girl or the mummy attacks."

"As long as you're working on the biography, too. I'll enjoy it. What did you manage on the train?"

"A lot about Egypt. Safi came out a lot sexier. What's the word from London? Anything yet?"

Edward shook his head. "Old Croucher has taken a hard line and since I have overspent myself, I must cease all expenditures at once until the first of the month."

Charlie calculated. "That's two weeks away."

"Indeed. I was explaining to him that should I be forced to remain in this hotel until the first, I will have overspent myself for June as well as May and still be unable to return to Harlow. I planned to remain there quietly for the summer. That should appeal to him."

A knock came on the door. "Telegram for Lord Withycombe." Charlie answered it. He tipped the bellhop and brought it to Edward.

Edward read the telegram and scowled. "Will cover hotel, train, ferry." He looked at Charlie. "We're not flying. He's dead set against plane fuel. Hates the things." He continued reading. "Return immediately. Lie doggo killer." He shook his head at the last three words. "Croucher has a liking for odd bits of slang and never hesitates to use them. I don't understand."

"The message says to hide out, stay low," Charlie interpreted. "Killer? Who'd you kill, sir?"

"What on earth? I need to get a London paper, right away." Edward dropped the telegram.

Charlie realized he had never really seen fear on Edward's face before as his lover hurried out. He settled back in at the typewriter while Edward went out for the *Times*. By the end of the second page he was worried. By the end of the fourth, he rolled the paper out, put the cover on, and went down to the lobby to see what had happened.

He found Edward in the bar, drinking straight whiskey, his face ashen. The *London Times* and the *Daily Mirror* sat on the bar beside him. When he saw Charlie, he raised his glass in a toast.

"To the dead man."

"My lord?" Charlie put on his stiffest, most professional attitude. Those loitering in the hotel bar at one in the afternoon weren't likely to speak English or even care about the situation, but he felt one of them should have some dignity. "Please come back upstairs at once. You had me quite worried. We can bring the bottle if you like."

The bartender tapped a bill grumpily. Charlie only vaguely remembered the exchange rate and dropped his last greenback on the bar. The bartender seemed to be satisfied. Charlie picked up Edward's papers and the bottle and took Edward by the arm to steer him back upstairs.

"I'm sorry, darling," Edward mumbled on the way up the stairs. "I'm not making the situation better. You'll already have to arrange for my bail because they're waiting for my return to arrest me."

"Arrest you? What on earth for?"

Edward waved to the papers. "It's all over the *Mirror* how I murdered you foully and Miss Brown and her cohorts saw it all. The *Times* just has a side note of, 'Noted adventurer wanted for questioning in death of American.' Bloody nice of the *Times* to be so circumspect."

Charlie lowered his lover onto the divan in their room. "Well, if it's me you supposedly killed, wouldn't the fact I'm still alive put an end to the story?"

"It should, but that doesn't mean they won't make a show out of arresting me." Edward sighed and leaned back against the divan. "I can see the headline now: RFC hero, Edward Kilsby, Lord Withycombe, arrested today for the murder of his secretary, American Charles Doyle. And the photograph, left to right, Constable, Lord Withycombe, Constable, and Mr. Doyle, looking very chipper for a dead man. And won't Miss Brown just laugh?"

"Better set it up with the banker. I've got twelve shillings, ten piastres, eighteen francs, two quarters, and about a hundred drachmae left. That's not bail." Charlie shook his coin purse and the loose change rattled.

Edward nodded. "Compose and send the telegram, please, my dear. Just in case the officers of the law are unreasonable. We'll promise to give it right back if not needed."

Charlie scribbled, crossing out and rewriting until the ten words said what he needed. "Returning Dover Tuesday. Need car, bail. Will return unnecessary bail." Edward nodded and Charlie took the telegram downstairs to the wire office to send it.

He returned to a thoroughly soused Edward and a half-empty whiskey bottle. "All right, Edward, I'm going to pack and get us ready to go home. We leave tomorrow. And you're too drunk to enjoy a night in Paris." Charlie kissed his nose and pried the bottle from his fingers, setting it atop the armoire. "It's all right. There will be other nights in Paris."

"We'll return soon, I promise. Let me rest. I'm not so very drunk. Damn Frenchman watered it. I might be better by dinner time."

"No Moulin Rouge. I'll get something from the market."

"No, no anything. I want you all to myself tonight." Edward reached one long arm out and snagged Charlie's belt. He pulled Charlie over to the divan and kissed him.

Charlie tasted the whiskey and squirmed under the big hands that were fumbling delightfully over him. "And you're a horny drunk." He kissed Edward's cheek. "Let me pack, love, and I'll be ready for anything you want."

"But I have to let go of you for that." Edward kissed him again and got one hand down Charlie's pants.

Charlie twisted away. "Yes, you do. Ten minutes, that's all. Watch me and think of all the swell stuff we're gonna get up to. At home. In Harlow."

Charlie packed faster than he ever had, glad neither of them were rummagers or strewers. From the corner of one eye, he watched Edward undress. He got them packed, working more and more slowly. By the time he had their passports and tickets lined up, Edward was naked on the divan.

Charlie gave up and went to him. He dropped to his knees on the floor and leaned in to kiss him, only to hear the snore issue from Edward's invitingly parted lips.

Charlie got up and got a blanket from his cot and covered his lover. He finished the packing, took up his journal, and made a few notes. He'd let Edward have a nap and wake him for dinner. Maybe they'd get their night in Paris after all.

Charlie wrote a while and then raided Edward's wallet for all the francs he could find. He left a note and headed out the door. Edward wouldn't mind.

He bought bread from a bakery and some red wine from the shop next to it. Cheese was cheap and he picked one that smelled nice, as opposed to some of the stinkier ones. A bit of sausage from the delicatessen and he was ready. It was much like shopping back in the city. As he passed a bakery, chocolate napoleons sent deliciously tempting tendrils of scent wafting to him, dragging him in to buy a pair. A nice dinner, all told, even if it wasn't pheasant with elderberry sauce or lobster croustade. He knew it was less expensive than the cabaret. The idea of a romantic picnic with his lover on the hills above Montmarte, watching the sun go down, appealed. The hard part would be waking Edward and making him hike up the hills. Charlie rang for the elevator. He'd settle for a romantic picnic on their hotel room floor.

He opened the door gently and set his purchases on the table. He went back to sit on the divan and kissed Edward. "Wake up, darling. I have dinner for us."

Edward snorted and came awake quickly at Charlie's voice. "Dinner? What?"

"I went shopping. We're having a picnic."

Edward scowled. "I hate picnics. Outside. All the damn bugs."

Charlie wasn't daunted. He'd learned in Harlow that Edward usually woke grumpy from naps. "All right then, we'll have it in here." He flung the tall windows open, letting in the sweet spring air and the sound of the street. He stole the blanket he'd covered Edward with and spread it under the window.

"I suppose I better wear something, before someone calls the gendarmes about an elephant in an upstairs hotel room. Wouldn't do to scare the old women."

Charlie laughed and spread the dinner on the blanket. "Just slide to the floor and come sit with me." He stripped his own clothes off. "If I can't be naked with my love in the privacy of a hotel room, I can't be naked anywhere."

Edward crawled like a hunting cat, his muscles rippling under his skin and his changeable hazel eyes burning greener. Charlie shivered just watching. Edward gave him the half-smile and settled down cross-legged to eat. The nap had given him an appetite and he complimented Charlie's choices in everything, even the wine.

They ate well and Charlie brought out the pastries. Edward ran a finger through the chocolate glaze and licked it. When Edward offered him a fingerful of the cream filling, Charlie moaned as he sucked at the long finger.

Edward smiled at him and leaned in for a kiss. Charlie gave it, more than willing. He clung for a long moment, losing himself in the chocolate of Edward's mouth.

They parted, Charlie breathing hard. "Love, if we do that again, we're going nowhere tonight." He glanced at the pastries and gave a soft groan.

"The night is very young, Charles." Edward stole a kiss and then took a bite of his pastry, the flakes of it catching in his mustache. "And so are we," he added, licking them away. He stretched. "Oh, darling. I feel much better. You take such good care of your feckless lord who wouldn't know which end was up." He finished his pastry and helped Charlie clean up.

Charlie kissed him. "You do fine, love. Ready for a night out? It's our last night in Paris, The train leaves at nine. Croucher has wired us five pounds for the train and ferry." He gestured to the sky, which had turned pink with sunset.

"Oh yes. I'm fully restored. Off to a show then? You won't run off to the loo on me?" Edward teased as he stood to draw the curtains and blinds before lighting the lamps.

"No, thank you. I remember last time. Besides, we're broke, aside from our five pounds and some loose change. It's been quite the adventure."

"Indeed, a bit more adventure than I expected." Edward lit his pipe. "And you… You've been dead and His Majesty's government still thinks you are. I am not looking forward to another arrest."

"Another?" Charlie asked, reaching for his notebook.

Edward chuckled. "As I said, I knocked around Europe and the Middle East both before and after the War. Alone, before. After, I had company, but almost never any money. I developed several bad habits most unbecoming of my station, slitting purses and food pilferage among them. Nigel and I became accomplished jailbreakers for these crimes, and I think we're still wanted in a couple of cities." He lit his pipe, the end of the Turkish tobacco fragrant in the room. "His lockpicking saved us when my charm could not. We made right messes of ourselves and anyone foolish enough to encounter us. But the worst was in Bucharest."

Charlie made fast notes, knowing he wouldn't put most of this in the biography. He'd try to make this incident sound like an isolated lark instead of the continuance of a bad habit.

"You must remember, Charles, we were just back from the War. Life at home seemed gray and dull, impossible to live. So we traveled and found trouble. We scarcely cared if we lived or died in those days, only wanting to feel excitement, to feel alive once more, as we had when flying." He paused, lost in thought and memory. "In Bucharest, we had been slinking through the city for days, sleeping rough in whatever abandoned building or cheap room we could find with the coins we'd been able to steal or earn. We were drinking that night, with some lovely young people—destitute artists, mostly." He looked at Charlie. "I'm telling you something I've never told anyone. Put your notebook away, this is not for publication."

Charlie obliged, sensing the story was about to turn awful.

"The young man was a dabbling sculptor. We three started home, him claiming he wanted, nay needed, to sculpt us, that he had been born to capture my face in clay." Edward spoke slowly. "Halfway to our room, we were accosted by the police. They didn't patrol the poor quarters often, the population was much too large for as few as they were, but tonight they did. They attempted to arrest us as vagrants and for being public drunks. We... resisted."

Charlie could almost see it. Edward would have waded in, fists flying, a manic grin lighting his face with the joy of battle. Nigel would have woven to and fro at the edges of the fray, striking here and there to best incapacitate opponents and aid Edward.

"When the dust and our heads cleared, our sculptor companion was as dead as the two policemen. The third lay unconscious. He recovered and we were arrested for the triple murder two days later. A fast trial left us awaiting an unpleasant death."

"Wow," Charlie breathed. "That's—"

"About what we deserved. We were fortunate the jail was several hundred years old. Nigel picked our way out of the cell and we ran for it. I'm possibly still wanted in Bucharest. Murder doesn't have a statute of limitations."

"No jobs in Romania," Charlie said firmly.

"No indeed." Edward rose and paced. It was still early evening, and Charlie knew it might be a long night if Edward had to stay contained in the room the whole time.

"We can't afford a show, but maybe we could take a walk?" Charlie suggested. "How about up to the big church? I've never seen one that big."

"I am hardly the man to talk about churches, but the Basilica de Sacre Coeur is a sight to see. Come along then, and we'll have a look." As they left the room, Edward said, "I never even asked if you were religious. I assumed you were Catholic, with a twice yearly habit."

Charlie sighed. "We were Presbyterian. My grandparents thought it best to leave all the quarrels in Ireland. I'm not much for church, and I never was. I figured you'd drag me along to Church of England services if we had to go. It didn't matter one way or the other."

They strolled up the street, headed to the large white cathedral that gleamed under electric lights. Edward finally broke the silence.

"That was past tense, Charles. Does it matter now?"

Charlie touched the cartouche. "Yeah. It does. Just not in the same way."

Edward nodded and said nothing more until they reached the park at the foot of the hill where the

Basilica stood. Charlie looked up and up, staring at the steps, illuminated only by the street lights. People climbed the long flights of steps, entering and leaving the Basilica. The great bronze bell tolled the eight o'clock hour, and some hurried a bit more.

"Do you want to climb up, Charles? You look a bit daunted. It is built on the highest point in Paris."

Charlie stared for another moment. "Then we should climb it just so we could say we did."

They made their way up the steps to the small park and then started on the next batch. Charlie tried not to show Edward how much this was hurting his legs and his lungs. He could do this. Other people milled around them.

They were almost to the top when a woman's voice called, "'Allo, Americain!"

Charlie looked up and saw a pretty brunette in a pink dress making her way down the stairs to him. She looked familiar. Before he could gather his wits, she kissed the air near each of his cheeks. Her taller companion smiled and adjusted her hat.

"It was a very long way to *le toilette, non?* But you returned to Josette, just as you said," she said.

Charlie finally recognized her as the girl in the red dress and stammered. She was apparently used to such greetings. She took one of his hands and pulled him down the stairs toward the public benches. He glanced helplessly over his shoulder at Edward who stood chuckling at the sight.

But Charlie noticed Edward didn't let her get too far away. He followed them subtly, keeping enough distance for privacy, but staying near enough that he could intervene. Josette's friend stayed nearby, also close enough to intervene, but not engaging Edward.

"You were sweet that night, *mon chou-chou.* Would you like to continue the sweet?"

Charlie shook his head. He remembered a very useful phrase from his French classes, one he had used on a couple shopkeepers that afternoon. *"Je n'ai pas d'argent,"* he said, telling her he had no money, that his pockets were empty of silver. A lie, because silver and copper were all they held. He hoped she wouldn't be insulted.

She laughed. *"Americain,* give me more poetry, and I will give you a kiss and we shall call it a trade, *non?"*

That, Charlie could handle. He recited one of his shorter favorites, in English, Wordsworth's "I Wandered Lonely As a Cloud."

She listened and smiled. *"Le jonquilles, oui?* Very sweet. I have read it in French but never heard it in English." She leaned in and kissed him, not the enthusiastic and deep kiss she had given him in the club weeks before, but a soft, sweet kiss, almost chaste. Charlie kissed her as long as she wanted.

Josette stood up and patted his cheek. "Come to the Moulin Rouge again, when there is money. I will look for you." She rejoined her friend and they continued down the long stairs.

Edward sat down beside Charlie, who wondered if he looked as stunned as he felt. Thoughts whirled through his brain and he stared after the women.

"We could have found the money, Charles," Edward said softly. "If you wanted her, that is. I worry that Miss Brown has tarnished the entire fair sex in your eyes."

Charlie shook his head. "We really couldn't. And I don't want her. The kiss was very nice, but..." he sighed, "I was kissed by a beautiful can-can dancer on a spring night in Paris, in front of a gorgeous cathedral. If this was a novel, I'd fall in love. Instead, I'm just kind of sad."

"What's making you sad, my boy?"

"I should have felt something besides wishing she was you." Charlie shrugged. "It was a good kiss, but I liked her smiling at me after I gave her the poetry better."

Edward nodded. "Do you still feel up to climbing the steps to the Basilica?"

Charlie turned around on the bench and admired the church, its travertine walls pale in the moonlight. "Not particularly. It's beautiful, but I think I just want to go back to our room and go to bed. We have a lot of travel ahead of us tomorrow, over two hundred miles."

"Probably for the best, my boy." Edward stood up and pulled Charlie to his feet. They took the stairs slowly and strolled back to the hotel, the gaudy nightlife of the district flaring around them. After a couple blocks, Edward said, "It's entirely possible you have no attraction to women."

Charlie shrugged. "Not too interested in men, either. Just you. I dated some girls—I like dancing a lot, and so many men won't dance that I could always get a date. But once I was out of school, nothing. Nobody appealed. Until you."

Ferocious yipping made them look around for the source, expecting to see a stray cat or something. Out of nowhere, a tiny fluffy dog appeared and assailed Charlie's ankle with ferocious growls. The conversation was lost and Charlie tried to not be bitten while Edward tried to grab the trailing leash, a feat made much more difficult by the way the beast kept circling Charlie's feet. Neither succeeded well and the dog got its teeth into Charlie's leg. That made it hold still.

A woman in a cloche hat with a colorful knot on the brim dashed up just as Edward detached and scooped up the snarling handful. "*Mon papillion!*" She cooed at the dog in a baby voice and looked at Edward. "*Merci.*"

"*Da rien.*" He handed the dog back to her, even as it tried for another chomp of Charlie. Edward hustled his secretary away from the inexorable canine. Once they were a block away, Edward slowed their pace and resumed the conversation.

"Most unusual behavior."

Charlie glanced down at his ankle, which was bleeding a little. "Weird. I'll need to clean up when we get in. As I was saying, it's you I love and you I want. Nobody else."

Edward looked serious and a bit worried. "I'm flattered, Charles, but that's a great deal to put on one man. You do understand I cannot promise you any sort of fidelity or exclusivity?"

"Did I ask for that?" Charlie looked at him sharply. "I know there will probably be an eventual Baroness Withycombe. I don't care about women or other men, just… have time for me?"

"Of course, always. Just so we are understood. Some people assume exclusivity and react badly." Edward let them into the room. "I'm not trying to be harsh, my dear. I just want everything clear and no nasty surprises later."

When the door shut, Charlie pulled him down for a kiss. "I understand. It's all nice and clear. I'm fine. Now, we've got a long way to go tomorrow." He wanted to ask Edward to take him to bed and show him how romantic Paris really could be, but their boundaries were established, and he wouldn't ask until Harlow.

# CHAPTER 10

# CALAIS, DOVER AND HANDCUFFS

Never doubt the power of words. The wrong word at the right time has ruined more men than all the wars and gambling parlors in human history.

—From the journal of Charles Doyle, secretary to Lord Withycombe

*****

Morning came much too early. Although they had shared a single bottle of wine at dinner and gone to bed early, they were still exhausted and nearly slept through the wake-up call. They made the Calais train with minutes to spare, Charlie glad that they didn't have to run for it.

Charlie sat on the train seat and opened his notebook. "Tell me about…" He thought for a minute and then shot Edward a smile, remembering last night and the Basilica. "Tell me about the first girl you ever kissed."

Edward returned the smile. "Ah…" He sighed. "It was a fine Easter morning and I was six, or maybe seven. When I was a boy, there was a superstition that if a woman wore one yellow garter and one black one on Easter Sunday, she'd be married within the year." He shook his head, remembering. "By that time, every woman, marriageable or no, wore the garters like that. She was five and so lovely. Hair like flax, eyes blue as painted china, and she had smiled at me all through church. So, on the church steps, I kissed her and started to announce my intention to marry her then and there."

Charlie laughed as he wrote frantically, trying to get it all down in Edward's words. The train lurched away from the platform and his pen blotted a corner of the page. He ignored the spot and continued taking the story.

"The grown-ups laughed. She burst into tears. Her mother hurried her away and all the other grown-ups laughed some more at little Edward, ladies' man. It didn't stop my father's hand from coming down hard on the seat of my short trousers."

"Poor boy. Did you have friends?" Charlie tried to make the segue smooth.

Edward shook his head. "Not really. I was the leader of a bunch of young rapscallions who were into every sort of mischief. My father's hand was heavy and he locked everything, but I was an accomplished vine-climber and lock-picker before I reached my tenth birthday."

Charlie wrote some more and watched Edward stare out at the passing French countryside. They moved in and out of patchy rain, the gray skies low over the fields and hills. "What did you wicked boys do?"

"Oh, everything. I had a reputation as an incorrigible before I kissed little... damn, I've forgotten her name. That wasn't long after the horse, you see, so the matter of me walking naked through town, nonchalant as you please, was still on everyone's tongue." He gave Charlie a grin. "And there was the little problem of the peaches coming ripe, but there being almost none because of a certain gang of greedy boys who climbed the trees and ate the best."

"You're terrible," Charlie said.

"I was. I was my mother's despair. I never stayed clean. I was forever tearing my clothes. I looked like a street urchin most of the time, not the baron's son. There is no way to stay clean and play properly. You can't catch frogs to slip into old ladies' baskets without stepping in a few puddles."

"I bet you tormented the girls," Charlie said when he'd caught up.

"And the schoolmaster. I can still hear him saying to Mother, 'The boy is brilliant, reads like a parson, knows his history forward and back, writes as if he were using his toes, and can't be troubled to learn enough to make him worth hanging!' I was twelve, then, and much more interested in the girls than long division."

Charlie took a deep breath. "Tell me about the girls."

Edward laughed. "They don't like frogs at twelve any better than at fifty. Especially not when the frogs are in their desks. Frogs were easy to catch. A snake… now that was a rare capture and had to be saved for exactly the right girl." He fell silent for a while and watched the rain roll down the train window. "I gave it up one afternoon. I'd dropped a snake down Louise Littlefield's dress. She shrieked and squirmed and I gallantly offered my assistance." He smiled at the memory. "I rescued the snake and Louise. She looked angry at me and said, 'My father will have you thrashed when he hears you dropped a snake down my dress twice.' Her face softened and she winked when she said, 'You do have time to do it again, don't you, Edward?' I can never resist a lady's request."

Charlie looked up, very dubious. "I don't believe a word of it. You probably started trapping every snake you could find just to get that reaction again."

Edward gave him an amused look. "No. After a few weeks, I took her someplace more private and introduced her to my own snake. She was mad for it. I understand she married rather hastily about a year later."

Charlie still looked skeptical. "How old were you?"

Edward seemed to be counting mentally. "Thirteen," he finally said. "Almost fourteen. Louise was only a few months older than I."

"Now I know you're pulling my leg. Try the other one. There's bells on it."

Edward shook his head. "I'm quite serious. I was a precocious child in every way pertaining to women. I was fourteen when Father sent me away to school, where I got my first taste of men's pleasures. I was not quite so precocious when it came to men."

Charlie closed the notebook, not sure he wanted to record this story, and stared out at the rain. "Who was he?"

"No one special. Just a pretty young man with a talent for the piano. There was no one who really mattered, until Nigel. School was simply fun and games and power struggles. Childish and forgettable." He looked glum. "Nigel…"

"It's what you said about the war. That you stayed alive to get one more night with him."

Edward nodded and patted himself down. "Charles—" he began, changing the subject. Charlie immediately handed him his pipe, tobacco, and matches.

"Thank you." Edward stroked his hand and started his pipe. After a few minutes of puffing, he sighed. "Yes, he kept me alive. I'm not sure if the same could be said on his end. He's incredibly hard to read, and has grown even more closed off since we came home.."

Charlie pocketed his notebook and joined Edward on his bench. He sat quietly as Edward wrapped an arm around him and smoked. They watched the rain wrap the laurel-lined lane that ran near the railway in a misty gray veil.

*****

They boarded the ferry at Calais. Charlie braced himself for the boat ride, but knew it was only a couple of hours. They rode topside, so he could have the fresh salt air. Sitting on the bench, the spray in his face, he could imagine he was back home taking the ferry across New York harbor. That helped a lot.

At Dover, the guards checked their passports and quietly hustled Edward and Charlie into a little room, away from the other passengers.

"My lord," began one policeman, "surely you've been hasty returning to England? You do know we have to arrest you for murder."

Edward nodded. Charlie protested. "It's my murder you're supposed to be arresting him for!"

The policemen looked at each other uncomfortably. "Yes. That does present rather a puzzle."

"Here, have a few more pieces so you can complete the puzzle." Charlie leaned toward them and opened his shirt. "Yes, Edward shot me, by accident. I healed up. Nigel Drake shot me, too." He dropped it off of his shoulders in the back, showing that wound. "That was no accident. I'm perfectly fine and willing to call it all a splendid adventure. Lady Sarah is a liar and a thief and I'll say that to any paper that comes our way."

The policemen looked over Charlie's passport, comparing his leaner, tanned face with the round and owlish one in the picture. They double-checked his British visa. Finally, they agreed there was nothing for it but to release Edward for lack of a single thing to charge him with. They warned him to lie low and let the scandal pass.

They caught the train back to London and on to Harlow. Robert met them at the station. "Pleased to see you home safe, my lord." He smiled.

Charlie settled in the backseat and didn't mind when Edward put an arm around him. He was pleased to see the manor house coming into view.

"I love adventuring. But it's always nice coming home again," Edward said. "Even to this dreary old place, where even the family ghost is second-hand. Now there's an idea. If I marry Miss Brown, I can wall her up and let her haunt it."

"Nasty, nasty," Charlie said. "You're already in trouble for killing me. Let's not be joking about such things."

"Right. Guilty until proven innocent and all that. Although having you argue my case makes a powerful proof." He chucked Charlie under the chin as they pulled up to the house. "Ever think of becoming a lawyer?"

Charlie didn't like the resentful look Robert gave him in the mirror. "Never. I'm content to write my stories and follow you around the world, leaving a little trail of used ribbon and paper." He added with a grin, "And half-drunk soda waters."

"Ah, good." Edward got out and Charlie followed. "I'd hate to lose you to the bar. And you'd look terrible in one of those silly wigs. Probably even worse than I do in mine when I have to sit in the House of Lords." He sniffed as they came in the front doors. "Oh my. Elizabeth has fresh peas for supper. Run."

Charlie caught his arm as he turned to flee. "It could be worse. Bully beef and Maconochie."

Edward groaned. "I miss Cairo already." He managed a few more steps toward the door and nearly bumped into Robert coming in. "Come on, lad. Hide us. We'll eat porridge, only spare us the General's fresh peas!"

Robert laughed. "I'm sorry, my lord. I was quite looking forward to it. There's some new potatoes from the greenhouse as well."

Edward stopped. "Potatoes, you say? Fresh potatoes?"

Robert nodded. "Dug 'em myself, I did, just this afternoon. She did up some nice cabbage and lamb chops." He gave Edward a smile. "Good to have you home, my lord."

Edward rolled his eyes. "Now I'm hungry." He draped one arm around Robert and the other around Charlie. "Come on, lads. Let's not disappoint the General."

Robert slipped out from under his arm when they came to the dining room. Two places were set at the table. "I'll see to the bags and the car, my lord," Robert said softly, ducking out the door before Edward could catch hold of him again.

Charlie sat down at one plate, where a pair of lamb chops steamed. A tureen filled with creamed peas and new potatoes sat between them. A smaller bowl of cabbage gave off its sulfurous smell. A nice bottle of Bordeaux sat by Edward's plate, breathing and waiting.

Edward sat down and poured them each a glass. "All's not entirely lost. We're home. There are lamb chops and good wine. And we're both safe and sound."

Charlie lifted his glass. "To many more adventures. May they be a little less hair-raising."

Edward clinked his glass to Charlie's. "Absolutely."

They ate the excellent cooking, although Charlie watched Edward pick the potatoes out of the dish and eat only those. They talked lightly of resting and enjoying the time at the house.

After dinner, they went up to unpack. Charlie settled his typewriter, a tad more battered and worse for wear, on the desk. He had just gotten his last shirt hung up when he heard the familiar yell.

"Charles!"

He hurried into Edward's room. "Yes, darling?" He looked around. Edward didn't need any jewelry. His pipe, matches, and tobacco were all quite comfortably reposing in a spotless ashtray near an armchair. "What did you need?"

Edward swept him into his arms for a kiss. "I needed you, dear Charles."

Charlie, reassured by this, lost himself in Edward's mouth. He'd missed the time they had enjoyed alone in Paris. The kiss went on, and he would have been content to stay where he was until supper, doing nothing more than kissing. Edward seemed pleased to continue as well. He guided them to the edge of the bed and sat them down, never breaking the embrace and pausing the kissing only enough to see where they were going.

The bed was more comfortable than standing and Charlie settled in for a nice afternoon. It seemed Edward was about to keep all the promises he'd been making the whole journey long. He had just looked up to confirm it when the tall window shattered.

The dead men poured through the broken window, seeming to swarm up the walls like lizards. Edward let go of Charlie and seized an antique sword from above the enormous fireplace.

Charlie grabbed a candle and a box of matches. He struck match after match, working to get it lit, but he fumbled them.

"Our adventure isn't over yet, it seems," Edward said.

"Apparently not!" Charlie called as he got the candle lit and set one of the mummies afire. "Don't let them touch you!"

Edward nodded. "Stabbing does nothing!" he yelled, wrenching his sword from between the ribs of the flaming mummy. It kept coming. He decapitated it and still the fiery body came, grasping blindly. The head rolled about the floor trying to bite anything in reach. Charlie silenced its snapping teeth by smashing it to powder with an elephant's foot umbrella stand.

Edward lopped the arms off of a second attacker and Charlie swatteded them in the fireplace with a handy umbrella from the stand. Then Charlie battered the body of the first one into the fireplace using the umbrella stand again. The dried corpse flared along with the arms. The armless mummy opened its mouth to shriek in silent rage. It lunged for Edward's throat.

With a crack, a blow from behind knocked its head squarely into the fireplace, leaving Edward sneezing from the dust even as he drew back from the attack that was no longer coming. Robert, wielding a cricket bat, gave Edward a smile as he shoved the remains toward the hearth. "One for zero, sir," he said.

"Good timing, lad. Keep scoring." Edward charged at the incoming mummies, forcing two of them back out of the window to shatter on the stone courtyard. "Damn. Impaled on Mother's favorite table umbrella," Edward grumbled as he decapitated another.

Robert kicked this one's head into the fireplace with a cry of, "Goal!"

Charlie made sure the fire kept burning. Robert batted another head his way and shoved the body back out the window. Edward chopped off anything that came in his reach, which very nearly included Robert's hand. "Sorry, lad, carried away."

"The ones on the train were easier," Charlie grumbled as he burnt the next two. The mummies kept coming until Charlie wondered if every corpse in Egypt had been pressed into service. The room was too warm from the fire and starting to get thick with dust from the crumbling monsters.

At long last, there was a pause. No more swarmed through the smashed window. Edward leaned on his sword and mopped the dust from his sweating brow.

"Thank you, Robert. What brought you here?"

"I saw one of them ugly beggars and mistook it for an escaped ape, crawling up the roof like it was. I grabbed what came to hand, dashed up the apples and pears, and arrived just in the nick."

Edward ruffled his hair. "Saved the old Khyber, too, lad."

Charlie was quite lost by all this, but Robert laughed. He slung his cricket bat over his shoulder, as if about to hit a googly. "I'll get Janine up here to clean the glass, my lord. It's a bit late to call the glazier. Olivia can make up beds in the study. It has no windows and only one door. As safe a place to defend as you'll find here, I'm thinking."

"Good thinking it is too, Robert lad. The trick is to be where they don't expect you. Have the car ready after breakfast. We're going into London tomorrow."

Robert gave a little nod. "Very good, my lord."

"He saved what?" Charlie asked after Robert left. He made sure the mummies were burnt to ash and blew out the candle. "And I didn't see any apples."

"Rhyming slang, Charles. It's rather like your gangsters and their colorful expressions. Apples and pears are stairs. The Khyber Pass is a place in India." Edward drew Charlie close and groped his rear.

Charlie rolled his eyes. "I get it. Khyber pass, saved my ass."

Edward nodded. "That's using the old loaf. There are dozens of such and a London Cockney in full swing is a lovely, if incomprehensible, thing to hear. He's picking up Molly's bad habits."

Charlie gathered up their nightclothes and pillows. Edward kept the sword and picked up a poker. Janine arrived with a little curtsy to sweep up the glass and they headed to the study.

Olivia bobbed a curtsy as Edward came in. Robert was building a fire in the great stone fireplace, although the night was warm.

"Should I stay, my lord?" he asked.

Edward patted his shoulder. "Get some rest, Robert. I'm sure you'll hear it if we need more help."

"Very good, sir." Robert bowed out, giving Charlie a little nod. Charlie looked at the pallet Olivia had made beside the couch.

"I like him. Good man in a fight."

Edward smiled. "Yes, he's a good lad. Certainly knows his way around this place."

"Cool as a cucumber, never blinked at mummies. You Brits." Charlie sent an affectionate grin Edward's way as he stripped down and pulled on the nightshirt.

"You're still wearing my nightshirt, dearest. I didn't see you blink, either, my cocky American boy."

"Yeah, but I've seen them before." Charlie stole a kiss and let Edward feel his nakedness. The hair was still not growing back where the manicurists had shaved him.

"We have to behave down here," Edward cautioned.

Charlie nodded. He sat down on the pallet and picked up the poker. "I know. That's why I'm on the floor and cuddling the poker."

Edward reached down and stroked his hair. Charlie pressed up into the gentle touch, the only one he'd be getting tonight.

"I love you," he said softly, stroking the necklace. "Isis and Osiris love me. And Anubis' boys have to go through me to get you."

Edward stroked him more and then kissed his fingertips, pressing them to Charlie's nose. "Sweet Charles…"

"Yes?" Charlie asked just as softly.

"Good night."

Charlie kissed Edward's fingertips before Edward drew them back. "Night, love."

# CHAPTER 11

# IN LONDON WITH DOCTOR WALKER AND LADY SARAH

In telling the truth, one must first gauge the audience and then the truth itself. Most people prefer a polished half-truth rather than a raw whole one.

—From the journal of Charles Doyle, secretary to Lord Withycombe

*****

The next morning, Robert took them to the townhouse and went to fetch Molly. Charlie settled into his room and patted the cover of his typewriter. He wouldn't uncover it until he knew for sure whether the mummy dust would be flying fast and thick here, too.

After a hasty lunch that Molly seemed to conjure out of thin air, since Charlie had seen that the cupboards were all pretty bare, Robert drove them over to Dr. Walker's place.

"You go talk to him, Charles. I have other business in London." Edward's eyes narrowed and his face went grim. Charlie felt a cold shiver and pitied whoever the business concerned. "I must see my backers and then Miss Brown needs a stern reminder not to cross me."

"Be careful, love," Charlie said.

Edward gave him a wicked smile. "I'll return from the university by teatime and you can watch as I turn her over my knee and thrash her. Is that careful enough?"

"No. Come with me or take me with you. That's careful." Charlie tried one last suggestion. "What if we're attacked while apart? Will you be all right? Will I?"

"I have Robert, and Jarvis is a ready hand with a cricket bat. Go on." Edward took a quick kiss on the cheek and smiled as Charlie climbed down out of the car. Once he was on the pavement, Edward waved. "I'll be back by teatime. If not, send in the Royal Marines."

Charlie watched the car drive away with a sinking feeling. He rang Dr. Walker's bell.

When he answered the door, Dr. Walker looked exactly as he had weeks earlier, with the exception of the sling and cast on his right arm. Charlie suspected he'd taken the faster sea route. "Ah, come in, come in, Mr. Doyle," he said. "Eddie told me he'd be dropping you by. Is he with you?"

"Uh, no sir, I came alone. I need to talk and Edward keeps looking at me like I was out in the sun too long down in Egypt every time I try telling him what happened." Charlie caught himself fidgeting with the necklace and stopped himself.

"Come on in, son. I don't guarantee I'll believe it, but you'll get a fair hearing."

"What happened to your arm, doctor, if it's not a rude question?"

"I thought you would know, since they trailed you back. I did my best, but that American ape—" He gestured to the sling and looked at Charlie. "No offense, Mr. Doyle."

"None taken. And please, it's Charlie."

Dr. Walker seated them in his study, a well-lit room with big, comfortable chairs and a cheerful clutter of books and paper. "Would you mind terribly making some tea? I'd planned to have some on, but this wretched cast keeps interfering."

Charlie followed Dr. Walker's instructions and got the kettle boiling. He set out the cups and sugar and milk. The tea ball presented problems, but he listened carefully and finally handed Dr. Walker a cup of tea. He took one of his own.

"Talk to me, then, Charles. Edward said there were difficulties."

"Do you want the whole story or the quick and dirty version?"

Dr. Walker leaned forward over his tea, a sly smile on his face. "Quickly, please, and with as many salacious details as you care to add."

Charlie told the story in as few words as possible, omitting most of what Dr. Walker knew. By the end, when he told of the mummy attacks just the night before, he was fingering the necklace again. Dr. Walker looked most unconvinced.

"Let me see that pendant you keep toying with."

"It doesn't come off, sir," Charlie said apologetically. He leaned close so Dr. Walker could read it.

Instead, the Egyptologist checked the length of the chain. Charlie knew it was too short to have gone over his head and there was no clasp or join. "Just as you said, on all accounts." He grabbed for paper and pen. "This is astonishing."

"What else can I tell you? How can we get rid of Anubis's men?"

"Tell me more about these manicurists. What did they tell you about the curse?"

"Nothing much, sir. Most of what I know, I picked up from a street storyteller and from Osiris. Ni-ankh-khnum is the more outgoing personality. He's kind of a flirt. Khnum-ho-tep is quieter, more meticulous. Oh, yeah. They shaved me. It hasn't grown back." Charlie's ears went pink. "Anywhere."

One of Walker's eyebrows went up and he muttered as he wrote. "I'll bet Eddie is having a ball with that."

Charlie blushed violently, as he had not since Paris. He stammered a bit and tried to clear his head with some tea. It didn't seem the time talk about that particular part of his relationship. "They were lovers, although both had wives and children. They were buried together. They kiss by bumping noses. It drives Edward nuts that I do that all the time now. There are days when I get up and paint my eyes before I wake up entirely and wash it off."

Walker looked up and smiled. "You haven't let him see that? You should."

Charlie blushed again. "Sir, please. We're a little busy being attacked by dead guys."

"Of course, I meant after we find a way to stop that." Dr. Walker laid his pen and paper aside and steepled his fingers. "Charles, would you submit to a hypnotism? Since your body was possessed, there might be remnants of the answers you seek still left in your subconscious."

Charlie hesitated for a moment and then, thinking of the mummies and the attacks, nodded. "All right."

"Make yourself comfortable, lad." Dr Walker searched around on his desk and found a small statue of Isis. He set it in front of Charlie. "Look at her. Follow her down, Charles. See how the light gleams. Relax."

Charlie watched the gleam of light on the goddess's wings. He listened to the slow, even voice. He dozed for a minute and then woke very relaxed, but in a state of unusually high awareness.

"Tell me of the manicurists," Dr. Walker said.

Charlie remembered everything, from the food at the feast to the feel of Ni-ankh-khnum's half-moon razor gliding over his skin. He told everything he could remember.

"I lifted their curse," he concluded. "They can be happy in the afterlife with beer and dancers, sitting beside Khnum the Potter."

"What did they tell you about the curse?"

"They didn't tell me much, they just bathed me and shaved me and got me ready to meet Osiris. They fussed over my hair a lot." Charlie smiled at the memory. He wasn't going to tell Dr. Walker how aroused the shaving had left him or of how Ni-ankh-khnum had kissed him.

"Did they tell you what would appease Anubis?" Dr. Walker pressed.

Charlie shook his head. "No. They never spoke of him." He heard Dr. Walker sigh.

"Did he speak to you?"

Charlie shook his head again. "No. He glared." Charlie hesitated. "I think he glared, it felt like a glare. He was mad I got weighed twice. And the heart-eating monster was really mad."

Dr. Walker sounded more excited and nodded. "So he was robbed of three he thought were his." He shuffled papers and looked one over. "It's very simple then. You must simply give him three lives in return."

"Simply? Who can die for that?"

"Anything alive, I would assume. I don't see why an animal wouldn't do. Does Edward still have chickens at the estate?"

Charlie nodded. "General Elizabeth does eggs every morning. But would a dog be better? Dogs and jackals and foxes belong to the Lord of the Embalming Chamber." Charlie covered his mouth, horrified that he could suggest such a thing. A voice not his rumbled out of his throat like a freight train. "This is not some decadent animist religion from Cush to sacrifice chickens. Mummify the dogs." Charlie shook with the force of the voice and blinked himself back awake. Dr. Walker sat staring at him. "What?" Charlie asked.

"Quite a phenomenon, dear boy. Anubis himself demands the dogs. I'll arrange it as a project with my students. A proper mummification takes about seventy days." Dr. Walker poured him a brandy. "You probably need this. I imagine serving as a god's conduit is a bit rattling."

The front bell rang. Charlie looked at the clock. Over an hour had passed while he was hypnotized. He swallowed a mouthful of the brandy, careful not to overindulge.

Edward followed Dr. Walker back into the room, looking downcast and tired. Charlie gave him a smile.

"Not a successful meeting, sir?" he asked. "Are we ready to go give Lady Sarah her spanking?"

Edward shook his head. "Not a bit. And yes, I'm looking forward to that. After all, I spent the afternoon being spanked by a dozen cranky academics." Charlie caught his breath sharply at that mental image. Dr. Walker chuckled.

"Shouldn't tease the boy, Eddie." Dr. Walker poured a brandy for Edward.

"Jarvis…" Edward sank to the sofa beside Charlie.

"I know you didn't mean literally," Charlie said softly.

Edward sipped the brandy and laughed softly. "Thankfully not. I just received a verbal spanking. It was almost worth it to see that look on your face, love."

"Bad, huh?"

"Terrible. They demanded I repay the money they advanced me. I told them to contact Old Croucher. I'm sure I'll come in for more tongue-lashing there."

Edward drank half the brandy and Dr. Walker refilled his glass. "Yours went better, I trust?"

Charlie took a deep breath and a slug of brandy for courage. "You aren't going to like the news from the doctor any better. We need to sacrifice three dogs and mummify them to placate Anubis."

The empty brandy glass fell from Edward's fingers and bounced on the thick carpet. Dr. Walker caught it before it could bounce again and break.

"I'm sorry, dear boy," Dr. Walker said. "I know how you love the beasts."

"That's just unacceptable, Charles. There has to be a different way to stop this madness." He turned to Dr. Walker. "Jarvis, what half-translated manuscript did you pull this bit of ridiculousness out of?"

"Just my own bit of hocus-pocus, my boy. I pulled it from your secretary himself." Dr. Walker helped himself to the end of the tea.

Edward turned and glared at Charlie. It was the first expression of displeasure Charlie had seen directed at him and it stung. "Explain, Charles."

Charlie fidgeted under the glare. "Dr. Walker hypnotized me. And while I was under, Anubis borrowed my body for a minute."

Edward rolled his eyes and Charlie winced. Edward was the worst man for odd moments of disbelief. That he should doubt the account was not surprising, but Charlie felt a bit wounded that Edward did not take him at his word after all they had been through.

Dr. Walker shrugged, a little sheepishly. "It worked. He is easily hypnotized, and that was not his voice that spoke from his mouth."

"Jarvis, you can't be serious. We sit here in a parlor with electric lights in the greatest city in the world and you're talking about ancient gods possessing my secretary."

Dr. Walker glared at him. "Edward, there are many things yet unexplained, even in our modern world. That you should fight mummies yet strain at believing in the existence of the being sending them baffles me."

"I have fought the mummies. They are real enough. I'm not ready to believe there is a musty old god with a grudge against my boy doing the sending. More likely we have some sort of artifact that's drawing them." Edward tried being rational about the situation. "Nor am I going to debate possession and divine revelation."

"What artifact? Edward, I have the cartouche and a few bits of jewelry the guys said I could have. Unless *you* pocketed something you shouldn't have." Charlie looked at him sharply.

"You were with me the whole time. Except while you were dead, of course. But you know I didn't take anything."

"Then it's Anubis. We have eliminated the impossible, so the remaining thing is the truth."

Walker chuckled. "I see why you keep the boy, Eddie. Now, we know what must be done. Are we finished debating who has asked us to do it?"

Edward held up his brandy snifter and Dr. Walker poured another drink for all of them. "We have more pressing issues. Finish up, Charles. We have a spanking to administer."

*****

They drove in silence to Sarah's house. Charlie felt like he should speak up and apologize for the demand that had been made through his body. But he could tell Edward didn't want to hear much of anything out of him.

Edward parked the car on the street and marched up the steps of the well-kept house. He pounded on the door, completely disregarding the bell.

Charlie followed him. He thought he was prepared to encounter their adversaries, but the sight of Nigel's high-cheekboned face smirking as he opened the door made Charlie step back down a step.

"Good evening, Withycombe," he said, not quite formally enough to be the butler, but much too formal for an old lover. "If you've come 'round hoping to mooch tea, I must warn you, Lady Sarah is abed with a sick headache and will not be taking tea or supper tonight."

Charlie could see Edward biting his tongue and cooling his temper. "When have I ever needed to mooch from either of you? Let her know I'm here. She'll change her mind. She always does."

Nigel remained planted in the door, an impassable barrier. Charlie realized how much smaller he was than Edward. Watching Edward's hands flex, he hoped Edward didn't decide to break Nigel in two.

"No, the lady is not to be disturbed. Be off with you and your sweet little catamite." He looked directly at Charlie for the first time. "Charles, dear, did you tell him about that magic night we shared off Naples?"

Edward gave a mirthless laugh as he seized Nigel around the throat and backed him into the house. "Go fetch Miss Brown, or I'll do it myself."

Nigel backed up against the solid bulk of Vincent. The big enforcer stood like a rock, filling the front hall. He said nothing, just folded his arms and waited for Edward to try bulling past him.

Edward eyed Vincent. "Well, well, and here I expected her to be listening behind the door."

Nigel twisted out of his hand. "Please. She's not to be disturbed. She's not well at all."

"Convenient," Edward sneered.

"Oh, do bugger off." Nigel's accent slipped a little, revealing his less-exalted origins. Charlie realized Nigel himself wasn't looking well. "It's bloody contagious, whatever she picked up. I'm barely on my feet after a bout. I hope I give it to you. Now get out of my lady's house!"

Edward laughed again and turned to go. "I'll see her within a week. Count on it." He opened the door. "Go on, Charles." Charlie moved out the door, but stayed close enough to hear.

Nigel scowled. He stepped a single step away from Vincent, caught Edward's sleeve and hissed, "I don't know how your little twist of American tail survived two point-blank shots, Edward, but I think you should know, I spent a great deal of time with him on the journey, the little dear, most of it not pleasant for him. Although when he expels, it is quite copious…." Charlie imagined a lecherous smile on Nigel's face and wanted to punch it. The man hadn't touched him, but everything he said was the truth.

He was gratified to hear Edward snap, "Liar. I was his first, I know. Nice try." It was technically true, even if they had been possessed.

Nigel returned, "Ask him. And I'll see you soon, my love. You'll need the lash soon enough." He paused a second and continued lower, "That little mole just above and to the right… you know the one. Do you think it looks like a figure eight as well?"

"That just proves you've seen him naked."

Charlie remembered his embarrassment of being naked when Nigel had taken all of his clothing to be cleaned and made him dress again when it was brought back. He'd tried to cover himself, but Nigel had taken a long look, with something that might have been jealousy on his face.

Nigel went on remorselessly, "Does he whimper when you bite his neck? Or have you yet?"

"You should know. You've overheard him with Sarah. Or did she invite you in to watch?"

Charlie heard a heavy thud and figured it had to be Nigel bouncing off of Vincent's chest.

As Edward stalked out, Nigel's voice followed. "I'll see you soon, love. The whips are already soaking so they'll be nice and supple."

Edward slammed the door of the house and stalked to the car. Charlie hurried after him. Edward drove recklessly most of the way home, leaving Charlie to clutch at door handles and seat backs as Robert held tight and winced beside him.

Charlie kept quiet. Edward's driving didn't need him as an added distraction. He hoped Edward would cool off a bit by the time they got home. He wondered if anything would come of his mentioning to the immigration police that Nigel had shot him, or whether it was even worth pursuing since it had happened in another country. He wondered about the taunts Nigel had thrown out about whips. He would ask Edward later.

And Sarah…

They hadn't seen the last of her, even if she was currently bedridden. Charlie knew she would recover and return to meddling. Legal repercussions were unlikely, beyond a fine for a false report. Perhaps a few well-placed words with the blind-item writers and yellow press would slow her down, force her to amend her reputation and give them some time free of her machinations.

*****

Once inside the town house, Edward pressed Charlie to the wall and stared down into his face. "Tell me the truth, Charles, did he have you?"

Charlie shook his head. "Not for lack of want or trying, but I was too sick. Amazing how quickly a well-timed heave all over his shoes will cool someone's lust. Especially a copious one." He turned Nigel's description around and gave Edward the truth of it.

Edward nodded. "He's a liar. Always has been."

"Not really. Everything he said was the truth. It's the implications that are the problem," Charlie said. He would have to remember that Nigel was tricky with words.

He pulled Charlie close and kissed the top of his head. They held each other for a long time in the hall as the spring evening came down and Molly rattled about in the kitchen. Only the savory smell of sausages and the whistling kettle broke them apart.

After tea, Charlie made himself comfortable in front of his typewriter and banged out a few pages while Edward caught up on the *Times* and the *Mail*.

When Edward finally put the newspapers away, Charlie began typing gibberish to cover the fact that he wanted to talk to Edward without eavesdropping maids. Edward leaned over the back of his chair and kissed his neck.

Charlie hit three keys simultaneously and they jammed. As he untangled them, Edward kept kissing around his neck and ears.

"I had an interesting afternoon," he managed, trying to keep his voice something close to normal as he resumed typing gibberish.

"Hopefully better than mine."

"I learned to make proper tea and got the 'You poor boy. Eddie left you out in the sun without your hat, didn't he?' look about twenty times. But Dr. Walker finally believed me."

Edward laughed softly and nipped Charlie's earlobe. "I'm sorry you had to overhear that scene at Miss Brown's."

"I didn't expect Nigel to be sorry. And good for you for standing up to him and not believing it."

"How good, darling?" Edward tipped Charlie's face up and brushed his lips.

"Very, very good," Charlie said and pulled him down for a kiss. After a moment, he stood up and let Edward steer him to the bed. The kisses turned long and luxurious, making Charlie's toes curl.

"Mmm, very good indeed." Edward kissed him more, grinding against Charlie until Molly knocked and announced that dinner was served and the gentlemen would be unhappy if they let it get cold.

*****

After dinner, they relaxed in the drawing room. Edward smoked and Charlie paced, turning the idea over in his mind, thinking aloud as he walked.

"We need to make some sort of canine sacrifice, then mummify it." He shook his head as he made the turn by the fireplace.

"Not my hounds," Edward said firmly. "I'll let Robert set them on you instead of the fox."

"Fox… Fox!" Charlie looked up from the floor as he drew nearer. "You hunt foxes." He stopped pacing and turned to Edward, beaming. "That's perfect. Foxes, dogs, and jackals are all sacred, so mummified foxes would be fine."

Edward mentally checked the date. "It's late in the season for a hunt, but I'm sure I could arrange one for the weekend."

He spent the next hour calling around. Charlie heard him argue with Croucher about the expense of a hunt. Charlie kept listening to the calls after that, to a club and then to a variety of individuals. Apparently, Edward was in arrears to his hunting club and they would not organize a hunt at this time of year anyway. Having been told no, Edward proceeded to call people he knew could ride the course. Charlie hoped he wouldn't be required to go. He'd read about fox hunting and it took a more skilled rider than he to stay mounted through woods and bracken and other rough country.

Edward hung up with a sigh of exhaustion. "I supposed I'd best go to the stables to alert Robert that we'll need Oscar and the dogs for Saturday."

Charlie nodded. "Want me to go tell the General?"

Edward smiled. "Clever boy. Please do," He was almost to the stairs when the telephone rang. Charlie stopped in the door to the dining room and listened.

"Hullo? Ah, Jarvis." He listened intently for a long while, his face growing more interested. He beckoned Charlie over and tipped the phone from his ear.

Dr. Walker's voice came tinnily from the receiver. "One of my students brought it in something quite interesting just today. We'd found that a lot of bird sacrifices were wrapped to appear as infants. But today, we unwrapped one mummified bird sacrifice and all we found were some rags and bone. It's of the same era with the rest. We suspect it came from someone too poor to afford a whole bird. Or some priest ate the bird and substituted the rags. So you see, Eddie, it need not even be one of your dogs. The intent is in the offering of the thing, not in the content of the sacrifice."

Charlie gave him a big smile and moved away. Edward chatted with Dr. Walker for a few more minutes and hung up. "That's it. We don't have to kill anything."

"You're the one who is talking to this god. Are you sure it's a good idea? Would fake sacrifices make him even more angry?" Edward asked. "Croucher will be thrilled to not feed ten extra people for a weekend." He rubbed his face with exhaustion. "And now I have to call them all back and tell them it's off."

"We could try making…." Charlie trailed off and a new inspiration hit him. It seemed to be a day for it. "What about a toy dog? That starts out in the right shape." Charlie thought a minute. "But, not just a new one from a toy store. It should be one that means something to us, so that it's really a sacrifice to give it up. I don't think," he broke off for a moment as if listening to something Edward couldn't hear. "Right, sacrifices can be made this way, but they have to come from the heart."

Edward nodded slowly, a thoughtful look on his face. "I think I have just the thing. But, I only have two."

"I'll have to get Toddy from home," Charlie said without self-consciousness.

"We don't have to do the mummification. We just have to let the students do it. But I… I want to do the praying part of it. I'm feeling responsible for the whole mess."

"We can wire your parents and have—Toddy, was it?— Toddy shipped express."

Charlie sighed, memory and childhood affection overwhelming him. "Toddy's my favorite. He was all brown and furry and I loved him until the nap wore off. But there comes a time to put away childish things."

"Especially when it will save our lives." Edward started composing the cable.

Charlie took over, barely able to imagine how to explain it. He decided he'd explain in a letter. "Send Toddy. Withycombe Manor. Harlow. England. Will explain in letter." They cabled it across the Atlantic, along with money for the hasty shipping.

Charlie shook his head as they came home from the telegram office, hurrying through the late London streets. "I'd love to be a fly on the wall when Mom and Dad get that one. They'll be terrified something has happened to me abroad and then puzzled. 'He wants his old toy? What on earth?' they'll ask. But they'll send it."

"I hope so. Or it may be us Jarvis's students get to try their hands at mummifying." Edward pulled him into the big bed and Charlie was too tired to protest that he hadn't even mussed his own.

# CHAPTER 12

# CURSE
# BREAKING

Gods are strange beings. Even after all my experiences, I cannot speak on the nature of them or why one will take a shine to a man while another turns his back on the same man. What I do know about the ones I've met is easily summed up. They like beer. They like music. They have warped senses of humor.

—From the journal of Charles Doyle, secretary to Lord Withycombe

*****

The wait for Toddy to arrive seemed interminable. No more mummies attacked, but Charlie had dreams he could barely remember in the mornings. He knew he was seeing Anubis, walking with the Lord of the Cleansing Room through dreamscapes of sand and stone. It felt as if the god was being patient with him for now, but should he fail in his duties, all hell—or what passed for it in Egypt—would break loose. He still couldn't go near the stables. Edward's hunting pack growled and bristled at him, a warning that Anubis was still unhappy.

Edward had produced, from a closed room, an ancient and tattered mother dog and her pup. Her nose had been sucked away and her ears chewed. The pup's tail hung by a few stitches, clear evidence of an affectionate toddler who had dragged it everywhere. One of its ears was threadbare. Charlie could imagine

202

his lover as a child, one thumb in his mouth, rubbing the pup's ear over his cheek until he slept, mother dog on guard against the terrors of the night.

The late post brought Toddy one evening near the end of May.

Charlie opened the box gently and brought out the seated brown and white dog, giving it a quick hug that he hoped Edward didn't see. He stroked the threadbare patch on Toddy's own ear and fingered the place where his once-fluffy tail had been sucked to a matted point.

They went into London the next day. They found the university laboratory and presented the toys to Dr. Walker. His students laughed when they were told they were to mummify the toy dogs, with appropriate spices and charms, and rituals and wrappings. They stopped laughing when Dr. Walker informed them it would count for half their marks for the period.

"These are the only dogs you're getting, Jarvis," Edward said firmly. He had expressed his worry privately to Charlie that the attacks would resume and they would be forced to use real dogs.

Dr. Walker just gave them an understanding smile. "It will be an interesting exercise."

Charlie released Toddy to one of the students with a last lingering stroke. "Maybe the fact that we poured so much of our own affection into them will be enough."

Dr. Walker watched as a couple of young men bore the three toys on a litter to an embalming table. A third wiped them with a barely damp sponge.

"I had Nile water brought in just for this occasion. It's good practice. It should only take the fifteen-day bandaging period rather than the full forty-day drying period, since they're already stuffed."

"The sooner the better. Anubis is getting impatient," Charlie said. Edward looked sharply at him and Dr. Walker studied him a little more. Charlie wasn't sure what the professor was seeing but the man made him feel like a particularly interesting specimen under a microscope.

When Edward opened his mouth, Dr. Walker held up a hand. "I wouldn't ask if you don't truly want to know, Eddie."

"I'm pleased they'll get a good sending on," Edward said. They watched a while as the students slowly began the wrapping process, including the first layer of spells, spices, and amulets. "Fascinating," he murmured to Charlie. "Doesn't seem like a bad way to be sent off, does it?"

Charlie giggled at the thought of a tomb like that of the manicurists rising from the back yard of the Harlow estate. Dr. Walker glared at him. Charlie managed to look a little abashed, but only for a moment. "Just imagine, though," he said, still grinning, "some renowned professor ten thousand years in the future finding these and taking them as evidence the Egyptians had Sears, Roebuck & Company."

Dr. Walker pressed his lips together to keep from laughing. He snorted instead. "I think it's time for you two to go. Any more of this and those boys will catch your silliness. Then the mummification will be all wrong and where will you be then? We'll call you when the mummies are ready, about two weeks." He escorted them to the door. "Eddie, being mummified isn't a bad send off. Except for the part where we pull your brains out of your nose with a hook. Good evening, gentlemen."

As they walked to the car, Edward pushed Charlie back against a wall of the university building in a secluded alcove. Charlie tipped his face up, smiling, hoping for a kiss. Edward tipped it back even farther and pretended to be going up Charlie's nose with a hook.

"Hey, if you want my brains, you'll need a big hook to find the poor little things," Charlie teased.

"It's all right. I'd only throw them away anyway. The real embalmers only worried about the heart, lungs, liver, stomach, and intestines." Edward gave him the kiss he'd been hoping for, keeping it quick and light. "Let's get home and give Molly the evening off, what do you say?"

"I say we leave my brains where they are and I think up new and exciting things to do in a big empty town house with a very handsome man."

*****

A little more than two weeks later, they sat staring at a trio of crates that Dr. Walker had delivered to the town house. Charlie had been enjoying London tremendously. There had been walks through shopping districts, strolls in Hyde Park to hear the political speeches, and Edward had taken him to the British Museum and Madame Tussaud's Wax Museum. They had lingered far too long in the Chamber of Horrors.

After a day of such folk as Dr. Crippen, Genghis Khan, and Jack the Ripper, they were nonplussed to find the delivery. Edward opened them to reveal three small sarcophagi, painstakingly painted.

"Woof," he said. "Now I have three mummies in my drawing room. Whatever will Molly think?" He turned to look at Charlie. "So now what? As Jarvis explained, we have to bury these at a temple of Anubis. Will simply having them ready keep things peaceful until we can return to Egypt?"

"People die everywhere. And your house, a shrine to death." Charlie gestured at the taxidermy and heads Edward had collected. Maybe they wouldn't have to travel after all. "The doctor is not right in all matters." The voice that he had heard come from his mouth once before now rolled out of him without thought.

"Charles, you've come over strange. Are you well?" Edward asked, blinking at the sound.

Charlie barely heard Edward. Other voices filled his head, telling him here would be fine, that the Lord of Death would wait no longer, that no journey was needed. He rose, unthinking, and went up to his bedroom. It was time. He made the ritual ablutions, washing himself as Ni-ankh-khnum and Khnum-ho-tep had. He could almost hear and see them, helping him in his preparations.

He dressed, eschewing the trousers and shirts in favor of a linen wrap. Slowly, carefully, he lined his eyes, a task he'd never done fully awake. He hadn't understood why he'd bought kohl at the chemist two days earlier. He'd simply purchased it on a whim and forgotten about it until tonight.

It was time. The phrase resonated through him, seeming to emanate from the pendant.

He went back down to where the mummies waited. Dimly, he heard Edward's sharp intake of breath. He moved the sarcophagi around until they lay in a neat row.

He dropped some incense into the burner shaped like a prostrate Egyptian slave woman holding a basket and lit it. Those, too, he had bought on impulse, not knowing why.

He sensed Edward come up behind him, but that was not important. Charlie dropped to his knees, ancient words from the prayers he had never studied coming to him with more ease than they should.

"Opener of the Ways, hear us. We beg your mercy." A wind from nowhere, hot and sere as the desert, rose in the room. The lights flickered.

"Conductor of Souls, we return to you what we have taken." From the corner of his eye, Charlie saw Edward sink into one of the large chairs, his face pale with fear, his eyes fixed on the center of the room.

"Lord Anubis, we offer to you our sacrifices, made from the heart and prepared with care." Charlie was unsurprised when the great jackal-headed god appeared. As he bowed, he saw Edward catch the poker in one hand as he sprang to his feet.

Charlie's heart quivered within him, remembering the touch of a deity's hand. He shook, overcome with awe, and prostrated himself before Anubis.

"Mighty Anubis, Lord of the Embalming Chamber, he who holds the keys of Death, we offer these to you." Charlie spread his hands to take in the mummies. "I swore to your brother, Osiris, that I had not killed. Nor could I kill to save my life from you. We could not take a life, so these are sacrifices that have been imbued with our own life-essence, the breath of the innocent. We give them to you to hold until the day we stand before your Balance again, our hearts to be weighed."

Anubis's hand on his head brought Charlie to kneel up. The pendant gleamed in the gaslight. He held still as Anubis took hold of it and read it. Charlie closed his eyes against the possibility Anubis would tear it from him.

Anubis closed his hand over Charlie's cartouche and held it.

Charlie could hear Edward shift, his breathing fast. He fancied he could hear his lover's heart racing. He knew if it was time to return his borrowed life there was nothing Edward could do.

Anubis released the necklace and laid his hand on Charlie's head in a gesture of blessing. The daze seemed to leave Charlie and he felt his knees want to knock. They would have, if he hadn't been on them. His teeth chattered although the room was warm. With the other hand, Anubis scooped up the three small sarcophagi and their contents.

Then he turned his attention to Edward. One side of the jackal's mouth curled in a snarl. He weighed the mummies in one hand and examined Edward, as if debating silently whether the sacrifice was enough.

Edward met the glare with a solid stare of his own. The poker in his hand wavered a bit.

Anubis cocked his head, looking for all the world like a gramophone advertisement. Charlie did not laugh.

Edward bowed his head a little, then gave a short bow from the waist, as he would to another baron. The expression that spread over the god's jackal face looked like a grinning dog. Anubis laid one hand on Edward's head, then vanished in a flurry of incense smoke and hot wind.

Edward sat down hard on the sofa, looking weak and drained. The poker fell from his slack fingers. Charlie rose and went to him. He bent down for a soft kiss.

"Is it over?" Edward stroked Charlie's face and pulled him to the sofa.

"It's over. My friends are free to go to the afterlife, and now we're free too. There shouldn't be any more problems with mummies. I hope." Charlie smiled at him, then suddenly realized he wore only a linen skirt. He settled in Edward's arms. "That was quite an adventure."

"Let's perhaps not have one so exciting next time?"

"Nope." Charlie stole a kiss. "And next time, I pack."

"Of course, darling." Edward's shakes were finally subsiding and Charlie curled in closer. He stroked Charlie's face and down over his chest and arms. "My own little painted Egyptian boy. Makes me feel like a pharaoh when you gaze up at me like that."

"Like this?" Charlie put on his most adoring look, the one he tried not to let Edward see because it felt too much like mooning about. "Yours to command, my lord and pharaoh."

Edward pulled Charlie's head over into his lap and stroked his hair. "Mine," he said softly. "My own beloved Charles."

They watched the fire and heard the London rain start to fall.

# AUTHOR'S NOTE

No book appears in a vacuum. The Curse of the Pharaoh's Manicurists owes literary debts to many sources, including Edgar Rice Burroughs, Universal Pictures and Boris Karloff, Indiana Jones and the recent Mummy movies. It owes to real-world sources as well: the Tutankhamen exhibit and the Egyptian room at the Field Museum in Chicago many, many years ago. The more recent Wonders of Egypt exhibit at the Memphis pyramid. The accidental discovery of a website devoted to Ni-ankh-knhum and Khnum-hotep.

Yes, the manicurists are real. Their tomb was officially discovered in the Saqqara necropolis in 1964. But there was evidence tomb robbers had found it well before that. So, I took a small liberty and let our unofficial adventurers find it as well.

We, the authors, owe many such debts as well. Cat Grant and Kiwi Carlisle, our early readers, gave us invaluable advice; Sue Rea (1946-2014) for encouraging us to make it longer (love and miss you, Mom); Sara Harvey and Stephen Zimmer for saying the nice things you just read on the cover; Fae Sutherland, Trace Edward Zaber and the rest of the Amber Quill crew for giving the boys their first home; and Kristi King-Morgan and the Dreaming Big staff for giving them a new home.